EARTHWORM GODS

SELECTED SCENES FROM THE END OF THE WORLD

BRIAN KEENE

deadite
press

deadite press

DEADITE PRESS
205 NE BRYANT
PORTLAND, OR 97211
www.DEADITEPRESS.com

AN ERASERHEAD PRESS COMPANY
www.ERASERHEADPRESS.com

ISBN: 1-62105-060-2

Printed in the USA.

Acknowledgements

For this Deadite Press edition, my sincere thanks and appreciation go to everyone at Deadite Press; Alan M. Clark; Tod Clark and Mark Sylva; Mary SanGiovanni; and my three sons.

Special thanks to the Wuller family, the Beauchamp family, Terry Tidwell, Chris Hansen, Robert Ford, Stephen McDornell, Tony and Kim at Camelot Books, Donald Koish, H Michael Casper, Nahed Shahabi, Scott Eubanks, William A. King, Penny Khaw, Leigh Haig, Paul Legerski, Robert Lewis, Phil Shepherd, Jamie La Chance, Michael Nolan, Trygve V. Botnen, Stuart James, Jason Houghton, Stephen Griglak, Larry Roberts, Mike Goffee, Brian Vaillancourt, Paul Goblirsch, Jade Rumsey, Kevin and Taya Locke, Michael and Karen Templin, Brian Lee, Robert T. Shea, Eddie Coulter, Edward Etkin, Michael Bland, Christopher Lee Shackelford, Drew Williams, Shane Ryan Staley, and anyone involved with the previous volumes whom I may have forgotten or missed.

DEADITE PRESS BOOKS BY BRIAN KEENE

Urban Gothic
Jack's Magic Beans
Take The Long Way Home
A Gathering of Crows
Darkness On the Edge of Town
Tequila's Sunrise
Dead Sea
Kill Whitey
Castaways
Ghoul
The Cage
Dark Hollow
Ghost Walk
An Occurrence In Crazy Bear Valley
Entombed
Earthworm Gods
Earthworm Gods II: Deluge
Earthworm Gods: Selected Scenes From the End of the World
Clickers II (with J. F. Gonzalez)
Clickers III (with J. F. Gonzalez – ebook only)
Clickers vs Zombies (with J. F. Gonzalez)

For Drew Williams,
a werewolf with a PhD.

TABLE OF CONTENTS

INTRODUCTION, OR, WHAT YOU NEED TO KNOW BEFORE YOU READ THIS BOOK

This is a book about the end of the world. Specifically, it's about the end of the world at the hands of Behemoth, Leviathan and their monstrous minions and offspring, all of whom previously appeared in my novels *Earthworm Gods* (also published as *The Conqueror Worms*) and *Earthworm Gods II: Deluge*. If you have not read *Earthworm Gods* or *Earthworm Gods II: Deluge*, then you should read them before reading this book— or at the very least, read the first book. Your understanding and enjoyment of this volume will be seriously hampered if you are not familiar with the original source material, and I don't have the ability to summarize 200,000 words-worth of plots in the limited space allotted for this introduction.

So, go read them. Then come back here. I'll wait.

Okay. Back? Good. Let's continue.

The majority of the stories in this book appeared in a previous limited edition hardcover collection also called *Earthworm Gods: Selected Scenes From the End of the World*. For the most part, the characters in those stories were based on real people. That is because the publisher, for a nominal fee, allowed readers to request a story be written about them[1].

I approached writing each tale the same way—I talked to the customers, found out a little about their lives and their loved ones and the places they lived, and then incorporated all of those elements into the story. I was very happy with the results, and the stars of the stories seemed to be, as well. I hope that you will enjoy them, too.

1: A similar collection with stories set in the world of *The Rising* was published as *The Rising: Selected Scenes From the End of the World*. That volume and this book share many of the same characters, since some customers paid to be in both. For more on this, see the introduction to that other volume or the story notes at the end of this collection.

In addition to all of those stories, this edition contains "Take Me To The River", a tale that was not in the previous hardcover volume, and was first published instead in the Lettered edition of *Earthworm Gods*. It should also be noted that I deliberately elected not to reprint one story from the original hardcover volume. I did this out of respect for the customers who spent an arm and a leg on the special collector's edition. Having that one story only available in the limited edition hardcover will help that volume hold its collectible value. Hopefully, you can dig that (especially since I included "Take Me To The River" instead). I also chose not to include the short stories "Earthworm Gods" and "The Garden Where My Rain Grows" because they were later reworked into the novel *Earthworm Gods*. For more on that, see my lengthy afterword at the end of that novel.

So, that's all you need to know, I think. I hope that you enjoy this short story collection. Thanks for buying it. I also hope that you brought along an umbrella and a shotgun. You'll need them both…

Brian Keene
June 2012

EARTHWORM GODS:

SELECTED SCENES FROM THE END OF THE WORLD

LOCKE'S ARK

Lafayette, Indiana

Kevin Locke was asleep when God spoke to him.

"KEVIN…"

He bolted upright, gasping. His wife, Taya, slept next to him, breathing softly. Their Yorkie dog, Harley, twitched at the foot of the bed, dreaming.

"Nightmare," Kevin muttered. He was about to lay back down when the voice spoke again.

"KEVIN!"

Kevin clenched the sheets in his fists and tried not to scream. A low moan escaped his throat.

"I AM THE ALPHA AND OMEGA." The voice boomed across the bedroom, rattling the lamps and furniture. "I AM THE LORD YOUR GOD. BUT I AM NO NIGHTMARE."

Kevin's heart pounded. He tried to breathe and found he couldn't. His ears rang. How could Taya and Harley sleep through this?

"BECAUSE I WISH THEM TO."

And the voice could read minds, too?

Kevin fumbled for the light and switched it on. Next to him, Taya moaned but stayed asleep.

The room was empty.

"KEVIN, IF I HAVE SATISFIED YOUR CURIOSITY, WE SHOULD PROCEED. YOU MUST HARKEN."

I'm dreaming, he thought. *There's nobody here, but I still hear it talking, so I must be dreaming.*

"NO, YOU ARE NOT. KNOW THIS, OH MAN. THE EARTH WILL SOON BE FLOODED AGAIN, JUST AS IT WAS IN NOAH'S TIME. THE END OF ALL FLESH IS BEFORE US AND I CANNOT STOP IT, FOR THIS

TIME, IT IS NOT OF ME. EVERYTHING THAT IS ON THE EARTH SHALL DIE, BUT WITH YOU, I WILL ESTABLISH A COVENANT. MAKE AN ARK IN YOUR BACKYARD. WHEN THE WATERS COME, YOU, TAYA, AND HARLEY SHALL HAVE SAFE PASSAGE. YOU SHALL TRAVERSE THE FLOODED EARTH AND SAVE MANY. YOU SHALL DO MY WILL, EVEN IN THIS TIME OF DARKNESS. HARKEN."

The voice stopped speaking. The atmosphere in the bedroom changed. The air felt less heavy.

"Hello?" Kevin whispered.

There was no response.

"Are you there, God? It's me—Kevin."

Silence. Kevin turned the light off and slept no more that night. He lay there shivering. The room seemed very dark.

He told Taya about it the next day. She didn't belittle him, and kept her tone neutral, but her expression was concerned.

"It was just a dream," she insisted.

"Do you really believe that? What if I'm losing my mind or something? I could be schizophrenic."

"You're not schizophrenic. Do you want to talk to Pastor Chad about this?"

He shrugged. "I don't know. He might get offended or something. He'd probably think I was crazy."

"No, he wouldn't. And neither do I. I love you."

"I love you, too."

Kevin had to admit, she was taking this pretty well. Taya was very religious, and attended the Reformed Church of America. Kevin had faith, but he had no patience for organized religion. He went to church with Taya, but he believed more in a greater good than he did in God. He considered himself lucky that Taya prayed for him often.

"You're not schizophrenic," she repeated, "but you didn't hear the voice of God, either. And this thing about the flood? God promised mankind that He would never flood the Earth again."

"He said this wasn't His doing, and that He couldn't stop it."

Taya smiled. "Well, there you go. If it was God, He'd be able to stop it from happening."

Days passed and Kevin chalked it up to a weird dream. He had three jobs. He worked for Custom Select Catering during the day and tended bar at Bruno's a few nights a week. He also operated an eBay business, selling horror toys and Bowen statues as Donkey Punch Toys, with his childhood friend, Shane. Between the three jobs and golf, there was no time to think about anything else—especially building an Ark.

By the end of the week, he'd completely forgotten about it.

God came back two weeks later. This time, when He spoke, Kevin was awake—sitting in his office, surrounded by books and Bowen Marvel busts and listening to the Boston Red Sox on the radio.

"Bases loaded," the announcer said. "Bottom of the ninth. Let's see if Varitek—"

The announcer's voice changed, exploding out of the speaker.

"KEVIN, WHY HAVE YOU NOT DONE AS I COMMANDED?"

"Oh God!" Startled, Kevin fell out of his chair.

"TIME IS SHORT. LEVIATHAN AND BEHEMOTH ARE ABOUT TO BREACH THE WALLS BETWEEN WORLDS AGAIN. YOU MUST BUILD AN ARK."

"No dream," Kevin whispered, cowering against a bookshelf. He clapped his hands over his ears and shut his eyes. "This is it. I'm crazy."

"YOU ARE NOT CRAZY. I AM THE LORD, YOUR GOD."

"Prove it."

"I HAVE KNOWN YOUR SOUL SINCE BEFORE YOU WERE BORN. I KNOW EVERYTHING ABOUT YOU; INCLUDING THINGS YOU DON'T KNOW YOURSELF. I AM ALWAYS WITH YOU. I WAS THERE IN BOSTON, WHEN YOU TOOK YOUR FIRST COMMUNION. YOUR PARENTS NEVER MADE YOU TAKE

"IT AGAIN. YOUR FATHER TOLD YOU THAT HE DIDN'T WANT YOU TO EXPERIENCE THE GUILT HE'D FELT AS AN ALTAR BOY. I WAS THERE FOR

"YOUR FIRST KISS."

"You know about that?"

"I KNOW ABOUT EVERYTHING. YOU SHOT A BOW COMPETITIVELY IN HIGH SCHOOL AND STILL HAVE IT IN STORAGE. YOU HAVE CALLED YOUR FRIEND SHANE 'THE PUNISHER', EVER SINCE HE CAME TO A COLLEGE HALLOWEEN PARTY DRESSED AS THE PUNISHER. HE HAD A ZUCCHINI STUFFED IN HIS TIGHTS. YOU AND TAYA WERE MARRIED ON SOUTH PADRE ISLAND AND SAID YOUR VOWS BEFORE ME. YOU'VE SPENT BOTH ANNIVERSARIES WATCHING THE PATS BEAT UP THE BENGALS IN CINCINNATI."

I knew it, Kevin thought. *God is a Pat's fan!*

"INDEED," God said. "AND I'M A SOX FAN, AS WELL. DO YOU BELIEVE NOW, OH MAN?"

"I—I don't know…"

The voice softened. "THAT IS OKAY, KEVIN. FOR I BELIEVE IN YOU. THAT IS WHY YOU MUST BUILD AN ARK."

"But I don't know anything about boats," Kevin said. "I mean, I can swim and shit, but—sorry. Didn't mean to curse."

"I HAVE GIVEN YOU THE KNOWLEDGE. ALL YOU MUST DO IS LOOK INSIDE YOURSELF. BUILD THE ARK, AND I WILL GIVE THEE A CHILD."

"W-what?"

Kevin and Taya had been trying, unsuccessfully, to have a baby. So far, Harley had filled that role, but Harley was a dog, and not as good as the real thing.

"God?"

The voice was gone again. Kevin stumbled to his feet. Like before, his ears rang.

"A baby," he muttered. "Build an Ark."

The announcer came back on, but Kevin was so preoccupied, he missed the final score.

* * *

Taya was at work when he decided to get started. Kevin called in sick to the catering business, claiming a headache. He got dressed and ate breakfast. Harley whined at him.

"You be quiet," Kevin told the Yorkie. "I know what I'm doing."

Growling, Harley waddled away and went to sleep.

Kevin and Taya rented a three-bedroom house with a small fenced-in backyard in a cul-de-sac that they affectionately called "Little Mexico." Their nearest neighbors were Rudy and Rosa. The house next to Rudy's was abandoned. Word on the street was that the husband was in prison, but nobody knew for sure. Across the circle from their home was a family with a teenage son, who the rest of the neighborhood referred to as Eminem. He hung out in front of the house in a wife-beater shirt all day long. To the left of Kevin and Taya's house lived a strange family with a pre-teen son who talked to himself and wasn't allowed to leave his yard. The husband and wife looked more like brother and sister, and the husband supposedly spent his weekends in Madison, Wisconsin, relaxing in the arms of other men.

Taya had come to the relationship with more tools than Kevin, so he had to borrow them from Rudy. No way was he going to ask the weirdo next door, and he doubted Eminem knew the difference between a hammer and a screwdriver.

He put on Dr. Dre's The Chronic—an oldie but a goodie, and then walked over to Rudy's house. When Kevin asked to borrow the tools, Rudy inquired about what he was building. Kevin shrugged. He couldn't tell his neighbor that God had commanded him to build an Ark. Pastor Chad would have probably said this was a wonderful opportunity to witness to Rudy about Christ, but Kevin was afraid that Rudy would laugh.

"A doghouse," he lied. "Harley's been crapping inside, so I'm building a doghouse for him."

"You don't say?"

Rudy's expression betrayed his thoughts. He was envisioning long, sleepless nights spent listening to Harley bark, wanting to come back inside. But he lent Kevin the tools. Kevin walked back to his yard.

"Now I need some lumber."

He paused. Dr. Dre filled the silence, rapping about the forty-four reasons that came to mind, why his enemy's brother was hard to find.

But what kind of lumber do I need?

"Who's the man with the master plan?" Dr. Dre asked.

Hell with the lumber, Kevin thought. *I need a plan. And I need to have my fucking head examined. What am I doing? This is ridiculous.*

He was about to give up and return Rudy's tools, when a cloud passed over the sun, casting shadows on the grass. Kevin turned his head to the sky. A single raindrop splattered against his forehead. Blinking, Kevin wiped it away, staring at the moisture on his fingertips. He looked up again. The sky was getting dark.

"Okay," he shouted. Then he lowered his voice. "Your will be done, God. Your will be done."

Thunder rumbled in the distance.

It started to rain.

NIGHT CRAWLERS

Montclair, New Jersey

"Are you crazy?"

Stephen Griglak looked at his wife, Eileen, and shook his head. "No. Why?"

"Have you looked outside?"

"Yeah." He shrugged. "It's raining. So what?"

Eileen stared at him. Stephen felt his cheeks flush. In the background, Bruce Springsteen sang about a woman in Calverton who put her baby in the river and let the river roll on. Outside, raindrops beat against the windows like bullets.

"You heard what they said on the news." Eileen sighed. "All of those poor people."

Stephen had indeed heard about it. It was all the newscasters were talking about. Yesterday, it had started raining all over the world. Worse, a series of super-storms were spreading havoc on several continents. Florida's panhandle and the entire Gulf Coast were instantly wiped out when ten-story waves crashed over them, driven ashore by a massive storm swell and winds of over two hundred miles per hour. Grand Isle, New Orleans, Apalachicola, and Pensacola were submerged in the blink of an eye, along with the two million people living there who never got the chance to evacuate. Interstate Sixty-Five, near the coast of Alabama, had been snarled in gridlock when it happened. All of those people died beneath the rushing waters, trapped inside their cars.

"That was down south," Stephen said. "We're in New Jersey."

"But it's raining here, too," Eileen protested. "It's raining everywhere. Just like what Al Gore has been saying."

"Al Gore is an idiot."

While Stephen believed in global warming (it seemed obvious that, in his lifetime, winters were warmer), he didn't believe its cause was predominantly manmade.

On the stereo, Springsteen gave way to Vivaldi's "Four Seasons." Thunder rumbled outside. Stephen wondered which season this was.

"Look," he said, "I know you're worried, but it will be okay. It's a freak weather phenomenon. Tomorrow morning, the rain will stop and the sun will be back out, and we'll be fine. But meanwhile, I've got worms to catch."

Stephen had planned a weekend fishing trip to the Delaware Water Gap National Recreation Area. He loved it there; the area had seventy thousand acres of ridges, forests, and lakes on both sides of the Delaware River in New Jersey and Pennsylvania. For almost forty miles, the river passed between low-forested mountains with barely a house in sight, before heading out to sea. Stephen loved camping and hiking, and knew how to fly-fish and track animals. He'd been looking forward to this trip for weeks.

All he needed was bait.

"You're not still thinking about going fishing this weekend?"

"Why not?" Stephen smiled. "With luck, the rain will keep everyone else at home and I'll have the river to myself."

Thunder boomed again. The lights flickered, but the power stayed on.

"I really wish you wouldn't. I don't think it's a good idea."

Stephen sighed. "Eileen, I love you. We both know what I was like before I met you. All those wasted years. We got married. Life has been good since then. But I'm in my fifties, and I want to do what I want to do. And right now, that's hunting for night crawlers so I've got bait for this weekend."

She glanced at the window. Lightning flashed.

"You're going out in that?"

Stephen grinned. "Yep."

Shaking her head, Eileen crossed the floor and gave him a kiss on the cheek.

"I'm going to bed," she said. "You'd better dry off before

you get in it with me."

"I will."

"And wash your hands. I don't want the sheets smelling like worms."

After she was gone, Stephen got a flashlight out of the drawer, and then found an empty margarine tub. He put on his raincoat, boots and a hat, and then stepped out into the storm. Cold rain lashed his face and hands, and the wind howled.

Stephen worked as a senior technician at an east coast university. He did soil fertility testing in their laboratory, performing various chemical and physical analyses. As a result, he knew what to expect in the backyard. Despite his assurances to Eileen, he was worried. They lived on a corner across from a small park, and their next door neighbors were ten feet away. Stephen feared that his neighbor's yard would flood. Water pooled there when it rained, indicating a clay layer deposited by the runoff from the retreating glaciers at the end of the last ice age. Their neighborhood was on the slope of a hill where there used to be a channel that drained the melt-water. He was concerned that if the rain didn't stop soon, hydrostatic pressure would force water up through his basement floor. It was already seeping through the walls, although he hadn't told Eileen yet.

Then he turned on the flashlight and forgot all about his fears.

They had a small backyard. There was a birdbath under a massive elm tree, and a large compost pile between the house and fence under a horse chestnut tree. All of this—the grass, the compost pile, and even the birdbath—was buried beneath thousands of wriggling earthworms. Their reddish-brown bodies squirmed atop each other.

Stephen dropped the margarine tub. "Holy shit!"

He'd never seen so many night crawlers before. There was enough bait squirming around in the yard to outfit an entire fishing fleet. Like the weather, it was abnormal. What could have possibly brought them all to the surface? Was there really that much water in the ground, or was something else driving them topside? A predator, perhaps, or a chemical imbalance in the soil? Whatever the cause, it didn't matter. Laughing, Stephen picked up the fallen container and stumbled into the grass. He took two steps and felt worms squish beneath his feet. Shuddering, he knelt and began scooping them up. The flashlight slipped from his grasp and landed with a soft thud atop the night crawlers. Stephen didn't retrieve it. He didn't even need the flashlight. All he had to do was reach out and grab a fistful. The worms squirmed between his clenched fingers. His hands grew wet and slimy.

"I am the great worm hunter."

Lightning flashed overhead, casting an eerie blue illumination over the yard. More night crawlers surged out of the ground. The container was full after a few handfuls. Stephen grabbed a plastic bucket and began dropping them into that. He cleared small spaces in the yard, revealing wet grass and mud, but immediately they filled with more worms. Then, over the downpour, he heard an odd sound—a gaseous belch. He glanced around, but the yard was empty.

"Hello?"

The noise came again, near the compost pile. Stephen grabbed the flashlight and stood up. His knees popped. He shined the beam in the direction of the sound and saw sudden movement. Something was burrowing beneath the yard, shoving topsoil and the mounds of earthworms into the air as it tunneled beneath them. It reminded Stephen of those old Bugs Bunny cartoons, when Bugs and Daffy traveled underground, searching for Pismo Beach. As it neared him, Stephen almost laughed. But the thing that exploded from the earth a few feet away from him wasn't a cartoon. It was a giant night crawler, easily four feet around. Its length was indeterminable. Much of it was still beneath the yard.

The creature's mouth opened. Stephen screamed. He stumbled backward, knocking the containers over. The captive night crawlers wriggled away.

Then the giant worm snapped forward and the hunter became the hunted.

UP A POLE, WITHOUT A PADDLE

Barnsley, South Yorkshire, United Kingdom

Phil Shepherd was grateful when his body finally went numb. There was just a slight tingling in his arms and legs. Nothing more. He was fairly certain the numbness was a bad thing, but at this point, it didn't matter. After two days sitting atop the pole in the rain, he was cold and wet and the muscles in his back, legs, and arse had cried out in agony until the numbness set in. Now, all he had to deal with was being cold and wet.

And the worms, of course. He still had to deal with the worms. They were still there, lurking at the base of the pole. They looked hungry.

Phil worked for Skanska UIS, a telecommunications company. His job was to put up telegraph poles and run phone wires to houses. It made for long, hard days—out early every morning and back home late at night, but he enjoyed it. One drawback to the long hours was that he didn't have much of a social life. At thirty-eight, Phil was still single. This bothered him sometimes, especially since most of the hair on top of his head was gone, and his goatee was showing its first signs of grey. But even without a girlfriend, Phil had ways to relax in his off-hours. He didn't drink, but he enjoyed watching films and reading books, or hanging out down at Riley's snooker club, where he was a member.

Another drawback of his job was that he often didn't keep up with current events. There was no time to watch the telly when you were running phone lines.

But even so, he imagined he'd have heard about the worms before this.

The rain he'd known about, of course. That was the whole reason he was in this situation. The storms had knocked out service all over the country. Worse, both the Worsbrough Reservoir and the River Dearne had breached their banks, flooding the nearby countryside. He'd heard that it was worse closer to the sea, but Barnsley was slap in the middle of the country. No chance of tidal waves here, unless they were of biblical proportions.

Phil and two other men had been sent out to restore service. Phil didn't know either of his co-workers. They were new to the company. One had introduced himself as Tim. The other was Simon. Both had moved to Barnsley from Wales. The three drove the crane and van to the site and then went to work. They'd dressed for the weather, but it did no good. Within minutes, they were soaked. Ignoring their discomfort, they'd dropped the wires off the old poles. Then they pulled the fallen poles the rest of the way out of the ground with the crane. Using shovels, they'd widened the holes and then used the crane's auger to drill deeper holes for the new poles. That was when they ran into trouble. The ground was too muddy and the holes kept collapsing in on themselves. Worse, the fields were full of other holes. Apparently, some sort of animal had burrowed up from beneath the ground. His co-workers thought that sounded reasonable enough, but Phil didn't know of any animal native to England that could make holes of that size. They were tunnels, really. Each one was big enough for a child to crawl into.

"Bollocks," Tim muttered. "I say we call it in and get out of this bloody rain."

"But," Phil said, "we were supposed to—"

Something long and white and covered in slime shot out of the nearest hole and snatched Tim before Phil could finish the sentence. The segmented monster attacked soundlessly, moving with a quickness that belied its ponderous bulk. The creature seized Tim with its toothless, yawning mouth and slithered back into the hole. His muffled shrieks echoed from underground.

Screaming, Simon turned to run, but found another worm blocking his path. It lunged at him.

Phil glanced around in terror and saw more of the monsters

closing in on them from all sides. For a second, he considered making a run to one of the vehicles, but before he could, Simon was swallowed whole. Instead of risking a similar fate, Phil scurried up one of the few poles that hadn't been knocked down by the storm. The worms wriggled closer, squirming through the mud, and surrounded the base.

And then the standoff had begun. The rain kept falling. Water gushed through the streets and began to pool in the field. The worms refused to leave. More of them erupted from the sodden earth and joined the others. A few of the creatures tried to snake their way up the pole, but slid back down again, lacking traction. Their stench filled the air—a cloying smell, similar to ammonia and chlorine and dead fish.

Phil wished for a rifle of some kind—or any type of long-range weapon. He was still wearing his tool belt, and had a claw hammer, screwdrivers, knife, and wire cutters, but none of those would keep the worms away. His cell phone didn't work. Each time he tried to call for help, he got only dead air. He kept looking for help, but none was forthcoming. The nearby homes were silent. Abandoned, perhaps. Maybe the residents had fled the storms. Or maybe the worms had gotten them all. The streets were deserted—no cars or pedestrians. He was completely and utterly alone up here.

Phil was hungry and exhausted. He wanted desperately to go to sleep, but each time he nodded off, the worms grew agitated, as if waiting for him to fall. He decided that he would close his eyes just for a little while—a few minutes, and rouse himself if he began to fall asleep. His breathing slowed. His head slumped forward, his chin resting on his chest. When he felt the pole lurch, his eyes snapped open again. Phil cried out, certain he was falling. But he wasn't. He hadn't moved.

The pole had.

He glanced down at the worms and saw what they were doing. A few of them had begun to tunnel beneath the pole.

"Somebody will come," he whispered. He was sure of it. His brother or sister would worry when he didn't come home. Simon and Tim must have had families, too. They'd be missed. Someone at Skanska UIS would notice they hadn't reported in. They'd send another work gang to look for them. Surely, the emergency crews would be out. The town was flooding!

The pole wiggled again.

"Somebody will come," Phil repeated, trying to convince himself. "Any minute now."

The ground around the pole shifted. Phil gasped. Thunder crashed overhead. The pole teetered back and forth.

He waited for help to arrive. The rain kept falling.

Then Phil fell, too.

ON THE BEACH

Morecambe, Lancashire, United Kingdom

The James family went to the beach in the rain—Stuart, and Nicky (his wife of ten years), and their daughters, Caitlin, aged three, and Antonia, aged six. Nicky had been hesitant at first. The news was bad. The BBC said water levels were rising all across the country. Morecambe had been experiencing high tide for the last twelve hours, and it didn't look like it would recede anytime soon. Going to the beach was folly, but Stuart had insisted. Earlier in the week, they'd promised the girls a day at the beach. At the time, the weekend weather report had called for clear skies, which in Lancashire, meant sidewalk-grey.

Now, the sky was more than grey and anything but clear.

Nicky frowned. "The beach?"

"Sure," Stuart said. "Why not?"

"Have you looked outside?"

He nodded, and then shrugged.

"But don't you think it's strange?" Nicky asked. "It's doing this everywhere. All of those poor people in Florida."

"That's all the way across the pond," Stuart said. "It won't happen here. Yes, it's odd that these storms are global, but it will pass. And we promised."

"Yeah," Antonia piped up. "You promised, mum."

"Can't argue with that." Stuart grinned.

Nicky rolled her eyes and groaned.

"Besides…" Stuart's smile faded. "You never know what might happen tomorrow. We should just enjoy today."

Neither of them said it out loud, but they both knew what Stuart was thinking. Antonia might have known, as well. It was hard to tell for sure. She'd been much younger when Stuart's illness struck, but she was a clever little girl.

Stuart and Nicky had been married for ten years, and Stuart was extremely grateful for each of those years. Nor, at thirty-eight, was he apprehensive about approaching forty. If anything, he felt lucky to see it. A few years ago, Stuart had gotten very sick and spent three weeks in the intensive care unit of the city hospital, and a further six weeks recovering in another hospital. Even now, two years later, he was still recovering from it. He didn't talk about his illness. His emotions were still pretty raw. But he felt very fortunate to be alive. More importantly, he'd learned to appreciate things. Sure, he still had his hobbies—reading and collecting horror books, watching football (Liverpool FC and Morecambe FC), and listening to everything from AC/DC to Bon Jovi—but these took a backseat to what was really important. His family. So if the girls wanted to go to the beach in the middle of the strangest global weather phenomenon on record, then that was what they'd do.

They put on their slickers and galoshes, bundling up against the rain. Caitlin didn't want to wear hers, and it took a few minutes to convince her. Then they went outside. Stuart carried Caitlin, and Antonia held Nicky's hand. They splashed through puddles, giggling and shrieking as the cold water soaked over the top of their boots. They didn't see many other people. The shops were open but empty. A single car drove by slowly, weaving around the deeper puddles. The family inside the car stared out the rain-streaked windows. The boot overflowed with their belongings.

Raindrops bounced off their heads. In the flat areas of town, yards and gardens were full of standing water, and the gutters and sewage drains were beginning to overflow. Water streamed down the streets and sidewalks.

It was a short walk to the beach. Morecambe was a seaside resort town located in the northwest of England. Sadly, it was a shadow of its former self. In its heyday, the city had been one of the premier holiday resorts in the country, boasting two piers, the beautiful winter gardens theatre, and an amusement park that had boasted one of the tallest big wheels in the world. All of this was gone now, eradicated—the piers and

30

the amusement park and even the big wheel—washed away by time. The glory days were over. Efforts had been made to restore things. The winter gardens theatre had been partially renovated. New coastal defenses had been built, along with a large promenade which provided stunning views across Morecambe Bay. Another new tourist attraction was a bronze, life-size statue of the town's most famous son, Eric Morecambe, who'd been one half of the famous comedy duo Morecambe and Wise.

Looming over all of this was the Heysham 2 Nuclear Power Station, where Stuart worked as a Plant Computing Engineer. Built right along the seaside, the nuclear plant dominated the landscape like the big wheel had done in years past. It made everything seem small in comparison—the town, the houses and shops, even the shore. But as they approached, Stuart thought the beach looked bigger than normal, seeming to dwarf even the power plant.

They halted. Nicky gasped. Rain fell relentlessly.

"Where did the sea go?" Antonia asked. "Where is it?"

Caitlin began to whimper, insisting that she wanted to go home. Her little body shivered against him. Stuart shifted her in his arms and stared out at the dark horizon.

"My God," Nicky whispered. "Look at that."

The ocean was gone, leaving behind dank sand littered with seaweed and trash and shells. The beach sloped steadily downward, shrouded in gloom. Fish flopped on the wet surface, struggling against the suffocating air. Birds circled overhead, gulls and albatross and even a pelican, squawking in shrill delight at the suddenly revealed smorgasbord. Far out on the horizon, shadows gathered.

Stuart tried to speak, but all that came out was a wheeze. His tongue and chest felt thick. His pulse pounded in his ears.

"Can we go down?" Antonia pleaded. "Look at all the shells! It's never like this."

She let go of her mother's hand and darted forward. Nicky reached out and grabbed her.

"Tsunami," Stuart wheezed. "We've got to go now..."

Nicky stared at him in alarm. Caitlin buried her face

against his wet coat, hiding from the rain. Antonia's attention was still focused on the beach.

"The ocean," Stuart explained. "When it goes out like that, it means a tsunami is coming. We've got to get out of here now."

Both he and Nicky glanced at the nuclear power plant.

"Can the plant withstand a tsunami?"

Stuart shrugged. "It can withstand the impact of a commercial airliner hitting it without causing a reactor breach, but a wave? I don't know. Worst case scenario, it might cause a massive radioactive release, which would send a radioactive plume across this area."

"We've got to go," Nicky echoed. "Antonia, come on!"

Overhead, the birds wheeled and flew away, heading inland.

"Mum! Dad! Look!" Antonia pointed out to sea.

Stuart and Nicky followed her finger. Stuart felt the bottom drop out of his stomach. The darkness on the horizon had taken shape and now it was coming towards them. The ocean had returned to claim the beach—

—in the form of a twenty-story wave.

Nicky's eyes glistened with tears. "Oh my God…"

Stuart held Caitlin tighter. Even as he turned to run, he realized that it was pointless. There was nowhere to run to. Nicky must have realized the same thing. She grabbed Antonia's arm and pulled her close.

"What is that?" Antonia asked.

"It's nothing," Nicky said, her voice quaking.

Stuart sat down on the wet sand, and called the others to him. Nicky and the girls turned their backs to the ocean. Stuart tried to smile.

"Let's draw pictures in the sand," he suggested. "And enjoy our day at the beach."

He started drawing stick figures—a father and mother and two little girls, along with a big sun. Nicky wept quietly. Antonia studied her parents' faces.

"I've got a better idea," she said softly. "Why don't we hold hands?"

"Anything you want," Stuart whispered. "Anything you want."

A siren in town began to wail.

They sat in a circle and held hands. As the noise from the onrushing wave grew louder, they snuggled closer together.

Then the darkness engulfed them as a family, and they were not afraid.

LAST DROP
OF SORROW
IN A BLUE BOTTLE

York, Pennsylvania

Bob Ford drank warm bourbon from a dirty blue bottle and thought back on the past few weeks. All over the world, it started raining at the same time. If that wasn't weird enough, the rain didn't stop. With it came intense super-storms that wiped out most of the world's coastal areas and killed millions of people. In the United States, coastal cities like San Francisco, Seattle, Los Angeles, Baltimore, Atlantic City, Norfolk, and Miami were all submerged within a week. Tornadoes and two hundred miles per hour winds ripped through the nation's heartland, leveling everything in their path. The rain didn't stop. The waters kept rising and the global destruction continued. Easter Island, the Philippines, Diego Garcia, Cuba, Jamaica, and parts of Asia were obliterated. Hawaii was nothing more than a few volcano peaks.

Bob watched it all happen on the cable news networks, until the power went out for good. He'd seen Denver buried under an impenetrable fog. He'd watched caravans of survivors heading for the Rocky, Smokey, and Appalachian Mountains. He'd witnessed the National Guard patrolling the streets of Manhattan by boat. A guy in Indiana had built an Ark in his backyard, just before the rains started. Bob thought that was a good idea. Wished he'd done the same. Apparently, some of the world's government's had followed the Ark-builder's lead, shifting their elite citizens and politicians onto battleships and cruise liners.

In Pennsylvania, the National Guard mobilized against this new enemy—the weather. Unable to shoot it or blow it up or fight back, they evacuated everyone in York. But Bob and Free Ride Angie stayed behind. Alone.

By the time the mandatory evacuation took effect, hundreds of people in York were dead or missing. That included Bob's wife, Jen, and their kids, Chloe and Carson. When the floods started, Bob was in downtown York City, working in the office even though everything else was closed and an official state of emergency had been declared. Jen and the kids were still at the house. The last thing he'd heard from her, before the cell phone network went down, was that the Susquehanna Trail had washed out, making it impossible for him to return home. The National Guard was there, urging her to evacuate. Bob had told her to go.

"You should be here with us," Jen said. "Instead of at work. You could die in there. They can't get into the city. The water is too high."

"I'll be fine," Bob promised. "Stay safe. Get in touch with me when you can."

But she hadn't. There was no way she could. The worst part was not knowing what had happened to them.

Bob took another sip of bourbon from his blue bottle. The warm liquid burned his throat, but he barely felt it, still lost in the recent past. He decided that the worst part wasn't not knowing his family's fate. The worst part was knowing that even if he had been able to get home, he wouldn't have gone.

He'd have stayed here with Angie.

Between the constant rain and the rising Codorus Creek, York City's streets were soon submerged. Bob took shelter atop the Strand Capitol Performing Arts Center, across from the county judicial building—the two highest points in the city. He'd seen a few people on the judicial building's upper floors, but had no way to communicate with them, other than waving. The storm's fury drowned out their voices when they tried to shout, and they were too far away to read handwritten messages.

He was alone in the Strand—except for Free Ride Angie.

And she was dead.

He'd known her. Not well, perhaps, but more than her other johns. To them, Free Ride Angie was just a whore and they were just customers. What they did together was nothing more than a business transaction. A fleeting moment of gratuitous, guilty entertainment. But not Bob. His relationship with Angie was special. She was his muse.

The men who came to Angie didn't know her story, but Bob did. He knew it as well as his own. It was an open book. She'd fled home at fourteen to avoid the attentions of her mother's boyfriend—not that her mother cared either way. The first trick. Facing the fact that the wet spot between her legs was what she used to live, at least until she learned how to give blow jobs. How she'd gotten her name—getting free rides from cabbies in exchange for sex. Bob knew it all. He'd created her.

And now she was dead.

He hadn't told Jen. She hadn't commented on it. But he'd heard it in her voice, before they hung up—the silent accusation hanging in the silence between them. Instead of being home with his family, he'd been here, at work, with Angie. Just like always.

And now Angie was dead. Maybe Jen, too.

Bob had another writer friend. After a night of too much bourbon, this friend proposed that the universe was nothing more than God's best-selling novel, and if the novel ever went out of print, everything would vanish with it. Bob had laughed at the time.

He wasn't laughing now.

He hadn't written shit since the rain began. He doubted he ever would. What was the point? New York—the heart of the publishing business—was a disaster area. The editors and agents who would consider his submissions were at the bottom of the fucking ocean. Who would publish his work? Who would read it? Why spend time scrawling stories in a notebook if there was nobody left to enjoy them? If a storyteller had no one left to tell his stories to, did he then cease to exist? Did his characters cease to exist as well?

Bob looked down at Angie's moldering corpse and decided that yes, they must.

She wasn't rotting. Something else was happening. Her ebony skin was covered with white fuzz. Some kind of fungus, Bob assumed. It was slowly liquefying her body. He wondered if he was breathing in the spores, and then decided that he didn't care. Death would be preferable to this.

He tipped the blue bottle back and drained the last drop of alcohol. Now he was empty.

For years, he'd sacrificed everything—everything—on the altar of his muse. He'd concentrated on writing, positive that eventually it would pay off, that all the hardships and dedication would be worth it, in the end. Fueled by booze and music and desire and drive, he'd written every day. Nothing else mattered. He'd put his family and friends and loved ones second, focusing on his work, conscious that he might lose them as a result, but hopeful that he wouldn't.

And now he'd lost both worlds.

The rage that had simmered inside of him all day suddenly exploded. Bob sat up in the chair and threw the empty bottle across the room. It shattered against the wall, showering the floor with shards of blue glass. He swept his arm across the desk, knocking the lifeless laptop computer to the floor. The casing cracked. Unsatisfied with the results, Bob lurched out of the chair and stomped on the laptop until it was in a hundred pieces. Then he kicked the plastic fragments and the broken glass all over the room.

His head felt fuzzy, his mouth dry. The room spun. He heard a terrible, high-pitched moan, and wondered where it was coming from. He searched the room.

Then he realized it was him making the sound.

Bob stumbled to the door and out onto the Strand's rooftop. The rain was much louder outside. It beat against him, streaming down his face like tears. He turned around once, staring through the open doorway at the fragments—blue glass and black plastic. Broken, just like him.

"Nothing left."

Bob walked to the edge of the roof and stared down at the street. The water rushed by like a river, covering the building up to the third floor. It would only get higher. Soon, the flood would wash everything away.

"I'm sorry," he whispered.

Then he leaned forward until he felt the world give way. Bob plummeted into the racing waters and drowned his sorrows one last time.

SWEPT AWAY

Cashmere, Washington

"So, this is how the world ends…"

Chris Hansen closed his eyes. The view wasn't what it used to be. Before the rains began, the window had looked out on a pond and waterfall about twenty-five feet away from their ranch-style house. Situated on top of a four-foot hill, the waterfall splashed over a pile of big rocks that his father had put there. It was one of Chris's favorite sights. When life brought troubles, watching the water was always soothing. Peaceful. It washed away his worries.

Now—not so much. Everything else had been washed away but his worries remained.

The hill was gone. The waterfall was gone. Everything was gone. Everything except the pond. With the seemingly endless rain, the pond had become a lake, submerging their square acre lawn and driveway and eroding the soil around the tamarack, pine, fir, and blue spruce trees in their yard. The water carried the uprooted trees away. Now, small waves lapped at the house, with no barriers left to impede them.

It wasn't just the pond, however. Cashmere was nearly eight hundred feet in elevation, but it sat nestled in a valley between the Wenatchee River and the Cascade mountains. Most of the valley had flooded already, filling like a bowl. Soon, their house would be submerged, too.

Chris's girlfriend, Francesca, had managed to keep most of the water out by stuffing towels into the cracks around the doors several times a day. But the rectangular house was built very low to the ground and within the last week, water had begun to flow into the crawlspace beneath it. Now the water was seeping through the floors and walls. The sodden carpet splashed when he rolled across it in his wheelchair. Mold crept up the drywall and the patterned wallpaper in the kitchen was covered with mildew. In another day—maybe less—the house would be uninhabitable. Then, just like the rest of the town, it would sink beneath the surface.

Eyes still shut, Chris tried to quell his emotions. This wasn't just a house. It was a home. It had become a part of him, just like the wheelchair. Chris was forty years old and had been a quadriplegic for the last twenty. He had good use of his left arm (except for the fingers), but very limited use of his right. He could not feel his skin or use any muscles below his collarbone. But he managed. He'd never let it slow him down. Never let it stop him from living. There were times of fear, of course. It was a terrifying thing sometimes, being paralyzed. But he'd never let the fear rule him. It didn't dictate his actions.

So why was he afraid now?

It wasn't the flooding that scared him. It wasn't his disability. It wasn't the fact that they needed to abandon the house immediately or the uncertainty of what would come next. These obstacles could be overcome, as long as Chris had Fran by his side. If the world was ending, then that was fine. He'd go out like Mad Max, in a battery-powered wheelchair instead of a car.

None of these things frightened him. But Chris was terrified of what he needed to do before they left this place. Of what he needed to ask Fran. It scared him in ways the apocalypse couldn't.

Chris opened his eyes. Fran glided up behind him and sat on the arm of his wheelchair.

"Taking a last look?" she asked.

"Yeah."

"We can't stay, Chris. You know that, right? The water isn't stopping."

"I know. It's not that."

"Then what is it? Why the delay? Are you waiting for Poe to come back?"

Poe was their black and silver cat. Chris called him Poo,

much to Fran's chagrin. He'd gotten outside two weeks ago and disappeared.

"No. I know now that Poo isn't coming back."

"Okay, then. We really need to get moving, Chris. Today."

"I know that, too."

"I've got everything packed. Food, matches, extra clothes, blankets. I put what I could into freezer bags. When the backpack gets wet, they should still stay dry.

He noticed that she didn't say, "if the backpack gets wet." Instead, it was "when the backpack gets wet." Getting wet was a certainty these days.

"How about water?" he asked. "Did you remember that?"

"Yes. It's weird, having to pack water when there's so much outside."

"That water's full of dead people and gasoline and stuff. I don't think we want to drink it."

Fran's nose wrinkled in disgust.

And that was when the three large skylights in the living room caved in with a loud crash, startling them both. The rubber seals around them had baked in more than a decade of direct sunlight, turning to dust. Chris had kept meaning to have them replaced. Now it was too late. The force of the rain had finally done them in. Rain poured through the holes, splattering across the floor.

"Okay," Fran shouted over the noise. "That settles it. We have to go. You ready?"

"Not yet. There's something I have to ask you first."

"Chris, the house is flooding! Can't it wait?"

"No, it can't. This is important."

She frowned, concerned. "What is it? Are you worried about the batteries in your chair? Because like I said before—"

"No," he said. "Not that."

In truth, he was concerned about the wheelchair. The batteries were almost dead and its movements had become sluggish. There was no way to recharge it without electricity. The combined weight of Chris and his chair was around three hundred and fifty pounds. Unless they were on concrete or asphalt, Fran wouldn't be able to push him very far. And where they were heading—there wouldn't be many hard surfaces. Water and mud, but no pavement.

But that wasn't what Chris was afraid of, either.

"What's wrong?" Fran's tone was demanding now. She'd obviously had enough of his stalling.

Ask her, he thought. *Jesus Christ, you've been together for over two years, ever since you met online. You love each other. What are you afraid of?*

Fran gazed at him expectantly.

"Will you…" Chris paused. His face felt flushed. "Will you marry me?"

Fran didn't respond at first. She stared at him in stunned silence. Then she smiled.

"What took you so long?"

"I don't know. I guess I was scared. I thought maybe you'd leave some day."

"I'm not going anywhere," Fran said. "I'm staying till the end of the world."

"I think that already happened."

"Yes, I'll marry you. But if we don't get out of here now, we'll never get the chance."

"You're right," Chris agreed. "No more stalling. Let's go."

Even though they were dressed for the weather, they were both soaked within minutes. Fran's long, dark hair was plastered to her head. She adjusted the wet backpack and pushed her bangs out of her face. Cold raindrops ran down into Chris's eyes. For once, he was glad his sensations were limited. Otherwise, he'd be freezing his ass off right now.

They headed for the mountains, seeking higher ground. Within minutes, they realized they'd never reach it. The wheelchair sank into the mud and refused to budge. And the water began to rise. Fran got behind the wheelchair and pushed, grunting with the effort. Chris stared over her shoulder.

"Chris, you've got to—" Fran paused. "What's wrong?"

Chris couldn't answer. He wanted to, but he was speechless. Fran turned, following his gaze. Her eyes widened when she saw it.

"The water," she panted, pushing again on the wheelchair,

"is it my imagination, or is it getting higher quicker?"

"It's not your imagination."

"Why is it rising so fast?"

"I don't know," Chris said. "Maybe something's pushing it higher? That's how it looks, anyway."

"We've got to do something."

She shoved harder. The wheelchair sank a few more inches. Mud squelched around the tires and sucked at Fran's boots. The water lapped at the bottom of the hill, creeping towards them. Another tree fell over, uprooted.

"Come on, you stupid thing."

"Fran."

"Come on!"

"Fran!"

"God damn it!"

"FRAN!"

She stopped her efforts and stared at him. Her bottom lip trembled. Chris saw the fear in her eyes. It matched what was in his heart.

"Fran," he said softly, "I'll never make it. Not in this thing."

"Then I'll carry you."

"You can't. I'm too heavy. You've got to keep going."

"I'm not leaving you, Chris."

"You've got no choice, Fran. If you stay here, you're going to die."

"Then I'll die."

"Don't be stupid."

"Don't call me stupid. I'm not going anywhere. In case you forgot, I said that I'd stay until the end of the world. And besides, we're married now."

Grinning, Chris blinked away more raindrops. "I don't remember a ceremony."

"There aren't any preachers left alive in Cashmere, anyway. But we're married as far as I'm concerned, and I'm not leaving you."

They glanced back at the house. The water was definitely rising higher—much faster than anticipated. Already, it covered the windows. The waves lapped towards them, gaining ground with every minute.

"Well…" Chris sighed. "This is one hell of a honeymoon."

He laughed. So did Fran. Then, without a word, she shrugged out of the backpack and let it splash into the mud. Her raincoat and shirt went next, followed by her jeans. Then she stood before him, naked, her body slick and wet, her nipples stiff in the chilly air. Sighing, Chris drank her in. His own body responded to the visual and emotional stimuli. Despite being paralyzed from the neck down, he was still capable of getting reflex erections. Judging by the look in Fran's eyes as she slipped his clothes off, he had one now.

"What are you thinking?" Fran asked, her voice barely a whisper.

"That I wish I could sweep you off your feet."

"You do, Chris. You do."

She straddled his lap, her legs thrown out over the arms of the wheelchair. Slowly, they made love. Chris nuzzled her breasts and throat and shoulders. Fran kissed his head and neck. It was perfect and sensual and romantic—and both of them felt like the first time all over again. Maybe it was that way for all newly married couples.

They kissed as the water lapped around the wheelchair's tires. Their tongues entwined. Fran pumped, driving him deeper. And when the water closed over their heads, neither of them cared.

They were swept away.

RUN TO THE HILLS

Minnesota—somewhere between Thief River Falls and Silver Bay

Paul Goblirsch and H Michael Casper (known to his friends as just H) headed up into the hills. Their progress was tedious. They carried a lot of weight, and the wet ground sucked at their feet. Paul was armed with a .30-30 rifle he'd looted from a sporting goods store. H had strapped a nine-inch fillet knife to his thigh and carried his trusty Ruger 10/22. Both wore backpacks loaded with bottled water, canned goods, ammunition, cigarette lighters, and other necessities. H's pack also held a water filter, hydration kits, batteries, a combination compass thermometer, compact saw, and a flashlight.

"Fucking ground is like quicksand," H said. "Can't find my footing."

"You're carrying too much weight." Much to Paul's chagrin, his friend had also packed an assortment of pointless items. "I don't know why you needed to bring all that crap."

"Like what?"

"The hairspray," Paul said. "The pens. The magnifying glass. What are we going to do with those?"

H grinned. "We can make weapons."

"Weapons? What are we going to do with a bottle of hairspray?"

"Turn it into a blowtorch."

"And the pens?"

"I don't know, Paul. Just keep walking."

They moved on in silence, climbing higher. The only sounds were Paul's labored breathing and the constant patter of rain.

"You need a break?" H asked after another mile.

"Sure."

They stood beneath some trees, rather than sitting down in the mud. The branches overhead offered little protection from the rain. The trees leaned perilously to one side, roots slowly losing their grip in the wet soil. Paul rested while H rummaged through his pack. He pulled out an energy bar and offered it to Paul.

"Eat this," H said. "You'll feel better."

H was in good shape. He lifted weights, jogged, and practiced Jam Jong-style Chi Gong and Ba Dwan Jin regularly. Paul's exercise regimen had not been nearly as exerting. Before the rains, he'd been out of shape and a little overweight. Now, with food growing scarce, being overweight was no longer a problem. But he had endurance in his legs and that was the important thing as they hiked farther into the hills.

Paul gazed at the valley below. "The water's getting higher. I can't believe—"

"How fast everything has flooded?"

H had a bad habit of finishing other people's sentences. Paul considered telling him to knock it off, but decided it wasn't worth the trouble.

"Yeah," he said. "That's what I was going to say."

"This is Minnesota. We've got a fucking lake every five feet or so."

"Not in Thief River Falls," Paul said. "I should have stayed there."

"You've got two rivers there—Thief River and Red Lake River. Both were over their banks when you left."

"Well, then I wish I'd stayed in Arizona." Paul had moved from Arizona the year before, to escape the heat and overpopulation.

"Paul, I goddamn guarantee you that Arizona is underwater. What we should do is make it back to my place."

"How would that be any different?"

"Silver Bay is about eight hundred feet above sea level. My house is five miles inland and a thousand fucking feet higher in elevation—surrounded by hills. The only way my property would flood is if Lake Superior filled up and rose over a thousand feet."

"Making your property the new lake bottom."

"Yeah. But that's not going to happen."

Paul glanced up at the dark sky. "Don't be so sure."

"Doesn't matter anyway." H shrugged. "Fucking roads are flooded between here and there. We couldn't get back to Silver Bay even if we wanted to. Not unless we find a boat. We're better off here. At least we're safe."

Instead of responding, Paul turned his head and listened. "You hear that?"

H frowned. "What?"

"I don't know. Sounded like a…fart."

"Wasn't me. I smell something, though. Like dead fish or chlorine."

Paul nodded. "Me, too. What is it?"

"I don't know. Could be chemicals or something. You saw all that shit in the water back in town. It's a fucking biohazard."

Paul finished his energy bar and tossed the empty wrapper on the sodden ground. Scowling, H snatched it up.

"You shouldn't litter. That's bad for the planet."

Paul gestured in a wide, sweeping motion. "Look around us, man. I think trash is the least of our worries."

"Okay, point. Let's keep moving."

They started off again, climbing higher into the hills. The strange odor seemed to follow them. A few minutes later, they heard the sound again—a high-pitched, staccato blast of air. Paul's description had been apt. It sounded like a fart. They blamed each other and laughed. It felt good. Although neither of them talked about it, both men had lost everything—their families, homes, book collections. After all they'd been through in recent weeks, laughter seemed healthy. It made them feel semi-normal again.

But sad, too.

Paul blinked away tears, pretending they were raindrops so that H wouldn't tease him about it. But then he noticed that H was also crying. He looked away quickly and shivered. It was cold. Paul tried to remember when he'd last seen the sun.

"We're gonna be okay, Paul." H's voice was hoarse. "Right?"

"We'll be fine." Paul smiled. "We just need to reach higher ground. Somewhere—"

"Dry?"

"Yeah. Dry."

Paul thought of their earlier conversation as they moved on. H's words echoed in his mind. *We're better off here. At least we're safe.* The peculiar stench grew stronger, almost overpowering.

Paul winced. "God, that stinks."

"Jesus…" H fanned his nose. "What the fuck is that?"

Before Paul could answer, something farted right behind them. They glanced at each other. Then slowly, they turned around. About ten yards farther down the slope was a seven-foot long giant worm, wriggling back and forth in the mud. The creature's rubbery flesh was grayish-white. Slime oozed from its pores. It had no eyes or sensory organs, at least not that the men could see. Paul gasped. His legs and hands felt numb. His ears rang.

"Jesus Christ," H yelled. "What the fuck is that thing?"

The worm raised its head. The flesh around the tip split open, revealing a yawning, toothless mouth. The farting sound blasted out of it. Then the worm slithered forward. It was faster than it looked. Paul and H scrabbled backward, fumbling with their rifles.

"Shoot the fucker," H screamed.

"You shoot the fucker," Paul shouted back.

Both men raised their rifles and simultaneously opened fire. They each pumped several rounds into the quivering creature, but it didn't slow. Brown ichor spurted from a dozen bullet holes. The men kept firing even as they retreated. Paul emptied his rifle. A second later, H's magazine clicked. The worm crawled on.

"I'm out," H cried.

"Me, too," Paul yelled. "Run!"

They fled. Paul raced up the hill, trying to avoid sliding in the sloppy terrain. He slid to a halt when H called out behind him. Paul spun around and saw that H had slipped in the mud and was sprawled on his stomach. His rifle lay out of reach.

H fumbled for his knife, but couldn't free it from its sheath.

The worm lunged forward and seized H's foot in its mouth. With a loud sucking noise, his boot disappeared down the massive gullet, followed by his calf. The worm's muscles rippled as it swallowed his leg. It reminded Paul of a snake eating a mouse. H screamed, reaching for him. Instead of grabbing his friend's hand, Paul strode forward. He flipped the rifle around in his hands. Holding it by the barrel, he clubbed the worm with the butt of the gun. The vibration ran through his hands. The worm refused to let go. Paul held the rifle's stock again and jabbed the barrel down, spearing the monster in its head. The steel parted the flesh easily, but then he hit a layer of muscle or bone—Paul didn't know which. Grunting, he shoved harder. Brown blood gushed from the wound. The worm shuddered and then lay still.

H yanked his slime-covered foot from its mouth.

"Holy shit," he muttered. "Damn thing was eating me!"

Gasping for breath, Paul reloaded.

"Thanks for saving my ass," H said. "I owe you."

Paul looked past him. At the bottom of the hill, a dozen more worms surged out of the trees and crawled towards them.

"Don't thank me yet," Paul said.

Thunder drowned out their screams. The rain fell harder. With each crash of thunder, the worms slithered closer.

"Son of a bitch." H glanced around, searching for his trusty Ruger 10/22. He'd dropped it when he fell. Then, the worm had attacked him. Now the rifle was gone. Worse, the tumble had aggravated his lower back problem. His spine and muscles felt like they were on fire. Cold rain streamed into his eyes, blurring his vision.

Paul stood next to him, feet spaced shoulder-length apart. He raised the .30-30 and squeezed off three rounds in quick succession. H couldn't see if Paul hit the worms or not. If he had, the creatures didn't slow. They continued crawling up the hill, leaving wide trenches in the mud. The smallest monster was about eight-feet in length. Rocks and trees crashed down into the flooded valley in their wake.

"Come on," Paul shouted, tugging his arm. "Let's go!"

"My rifle," H yelled. "Where the hell is it?"

"The mud must have sucked it down. Forget about it. We've still got mine. Hurry up."

"We need the fucking gun!"

"Forget about the goddamned gun! Look behind us. Now let's—"

"Go?" H asked, finishing Paul's sentence. "Not yet. I'm not leaving that rifle behind."

Thunder boomed again. The worms moved in silence, closing the distance.

"You've still got the knife," Paul said. "And all that other stuff—the pens and the hairspray. You said we could use them as weapons."

"Sure, but not now! What the hell am I gonna do with a pen against those fucking things? Stab them in the eye? They don't have eyes. They don't have anything—just big, hungry mouths. What the fuck is a pen or hairspray going to do against that?"

"Well, excuse me, MacGyver! I didn't know your special weapons were reserved for specific threats."

H clawed at the wet topsoil, scooping aside handfuls of mud, searching for the rifle. He tried to ignore the searing pain in his back.

"It's gone," he moaned. "Shit, I can't believe I lost it."

"Please," Paul urged. "They're almost on us! We've got to go now. Forget about the gun, H. I promise, I'll steal you a new one when we find another hardware store. Anything you want. An M-16. A grenade launcher. Just get up!"

Paul fired another shot while H stumbled to his feet. Then they continued up the hill. They didn't run. They couldn't. The terrain had become too slippery. With each step, their boots sank into the mud, slowing their progress. Paul reloaded as they went. H gritted his teeth, trying to ignore the pain in his back.

"Maybe we should lose the backpacks," Paul suggested, gasping for breath.

H shook his head. "Can't. All our food and the first aid kit are in them. We just need to find solid ground—somewhere to make a stand."

Suddenly, the hillside rumbled beneath their feet. H grabbed a sapling, fighting to keep his balance, and saw movement out of the corner of his eye. He turned to the right and saw a furrow of wet topsoil moving towards them. Something was burrowing beneath the surface. Judging from the size of the mound, it wasn't a gopher.

A massive grayish-white tube of rubbery flesh exploded from the ground, sending mud and rocks showering down upon them. The worm's tip split open, and the now-familiar farting noise blasted out of its toothless mouth. This monster dwarfed the other pursuers. Paul tried to run, tumbling through the mud, but H held his ground. The worm's upper half towered over him, looming high enough to block the rain. It swayed back and forth. Ignoring the imminent danger, H studied the creature, analyzing it with his biology-trained mind. Like the others, it had no eyes or sensory organs. How, then, did it know they were here?

"H!"

Paul's scream broke his silent reverie. Behind them, the rampaging worms were now just yards away. Slipping his knife from its sheath, H glanced back up at the larger worm in front of him. Its lower half was still in the ground. The rest cast a shadow over him. Slime dripped from its pores, splattering against his coat in time with the rain. Mouth gaping, the creature lunged downward.

H had already been inside one of these things today. He had no intention of going through it again. He winced as the mouth neared him. The worm's breath was hot and fetid. H slashed at the sickly flesh with his knife. The blade sank deep. Warm, brown fluid gushed from the wound and splashed over H's hand and wrist. Hissing, the creature reared backward and then disappeared back into the ground. Behind them, the other worms paused.

"They're communal," H shouted. "One of them got hurt, and the others sensed it. Now they're wary."

"So?"

"It means they're intelligent."

"So are sharks," Paul shouted. "That doesn't stop them from eating you."

"Look." H pointed at the quivering worms. "They're not retreating but neither are they moving forward.

Paul frowned. "How does that—?"

"Help us?" H interrupted him. "It buys us some time. Come on, we've got to go!"

"That's what I've been saying all along."

They plodded on, using wide, loping strides and fighting for balance. The rain poured harder, obscuring everything more than a few feet away. Worse, what little daylight they'd had left—the pale rays that managed to filter through the nearly impenetrable cloud cover—now faded, plunging the hillside into darkness. H reached for Paul's hand and squeezed it.

Paul tried to pull away. "What are you—"

"Oh, knock it off. The rain's coming down in sheets. We can't see shit. This is so we don't lose each other."

They paused, listening for sounds of pursuit, but all they heard was the steady downpour—huge drops smacking against wet earth, splashing into puddles, drumming against the dying vegetation.

"Do you think they're gone?" Paul asked.

H didn't respond. Instead, he led his friend forward into the gloom. As they trudged along, he thought of his wife, Eileen. Could she still be alive, somewhere out there? Probably not. She'd worked at the public library in town—much closer to Lake Superior than their home had been. The Federal Emergency Management Agency had set up a shelter there, aiding flood victims. A week after the rains started, Eileen had been helping out. An armored National Guard Humvee had picked her up at the house and taken her in with some of the other volunteers.

She'd never come home.

When H attempted to search for her, the town no longer existed. It had been replaced by a newly enlarged Lake Superior. And his home, previously five miles above it, became lakeside property. Then Paul had shown up, and the two had banded together, retreating from the rising floodwaters.

Nowhere to go but up…

H felt Paul stop suddenly. He squeezed H's hand hard enough to make him wince.

"You okay?" H asked.

"Look," Paul whispered. "Is that what I think it is?"

"Where? I can't see shit out here, man."

"To our left. Near the top of the hill."

H peered into the shadows. After a moment, he saw it—a black hole in the hillside, situated between two large boulders. A cave.

"Son of a bitch…Come on!"

Still clutching hands, they hurried towards the entrance. It was about four and a half feet in diameter and roughly circular. A small stream of water trickled through the opening and disappeared inside. It appeared as if the cave slanted downward.

H turned his back to Paul. "Reach in my backpack and get the flashlight."

Paul fumbled with the wet straps and dug through the backpack. "I can't find it. You've got too much stuff and it's too dark. Let's get inside first."

"Screw that. I'm not going in without a flashlight. What if there's a raccoon or a bear or something?"

"Well," Paul said, "I'd prefer that to those worm-things."

"Point. But you go first."

Sighing, Paul dropped to his hands and knees and crawled through the entrance. H followed after him. The tunnel sloped steadily downward, leading deep beneath the hills. The walls and floor felt slimy, and the air reeked faintly of chlorine. After a few minutes, H called a stop. They huddled together in the darkness.

"Okay," H whispered. "I think we're safe for the time being. Feels good to be out of that rain, doesn't it?"

"Yeah," Paul agreed. "It does."

H wiped his hands on his wet shirt. "Wonder what this shit is all over the floor and walls? It stinks."

"Feels like snot," Paul said.

"Let me get the flashlight out and we'll see about making camp."

"In here?"

"Sure," H said. "Why not? It's dryer and safer than sleeping outside."

"Think we can make a fire?"

"Maybe. At the very least, we can dry off a bit, and eat something. I just wish we had some spicy Asian takeout. Wonder if we can find a place that will deliver?"

Paul snickered. The sound made H feel better. He slid out of his backpack and rummaged through it, searching for the flashlight. His fingers closed on a single, warm bottle of Spaten Optimator. Surprisingly, it had survived the fall and hadn't broken. He pulled the beer out and sat it aside for later. Then he stuck his hand back in the pack and found the light.

He clicked it on.

Shined it around.

Screamed.

A giant worm sat ten feet away from them. Its massive girth blocked the entire tunnel.

"Outside," H shouted. "Go, go, go!"

He and Paul frantically turned, scurrying back towards the entrance, only to find it was blocked, as well. Worms surged through the opening. They were surrounded.

"This wasn't a cave," H whispered, pulling out his knife. "Motherfucker…"

"What do we do?" Paul yelled.

H laughed. "You know, Albert Einstein once said that only two things are infinite."

Paul gaped at him as if he'd lost his mind.

"Those things," H continued, "are the universe and human stupidity, and I'm not sure about the former."

His laughter echoed down the tunnel, accompanying Paul's screams, as the worms slithered closer.

FLOATING HOME

Somewhere in the New Pacific

Terry Tidwell looked down into the depths and thought of home. It was somewhere down there, far below. Maybe not right at this spot. Without navigational equipment, he couldn't be sure of his exact location. He was floating above Fort Bragg. Or maybe Noyo. Or Westport. Or MacKerricher State Park or Willits or somewhere else along the Pacific coastline. It was hard to tell with everything submerged. His only markers were the occasional tip of a cell phone tower or redwood tree jutting above the waves.

Home. He needed to stop thinking about it. Doing so made his stomach hurt. It was gone—down there at the bottom of the ocean along with everything else. This was his home now. This makeshift raft, built from housing timbers and telephone poles, and lashed together with rope, steel cables, and extension cords—anything that would work. Atop the platform were three portable toilets that he'd recovered from a construction site. These were tied down to prevent them from falling into the ocean. One of them still retained its original function. The second held the few supplies and personal belongings he'd managed to rescue before the flood—fresh water, canned goods, a case of Fosters Lager, cigarette lighters, kerosene, books, clothing, and his old .30-30 rifle. The third toilet was where Terry and Woody, his Jack Russell Terrier, slept— cramped and uncomfortable, but dry.

Terry looked down at Woody. "This is the life, huh?"

The dog responded by shaking himself, spraying water in every direction. Terry flinched, recoiling out of habit. Then he laughed.

"Guess I can't get any wetter than I already am."

Nothing better defined luxury these days than a dry place to rest, because dryness—like his home and family and friends—had ceased to exist. Now there was just the rain, ever-present and unavoidably soaking. That was why both he and Woody spent most of their time inside the portable toilet. He'd only been out here a few minutes, long enough to travel between the storage john and his sleeping quarters, but already he was drenched. In addition to the rain, there was the constant spray of salty seawater. Droplets fell from his nose and hair. Terry shivered.

Woody barked twice. The dog was staring at the horizon. Terry followed his gaze.

A boat was approaching. He heard the distant drone of a motor. Unlike him, they weren't drifting aimlessly on the current. The vessel also had a sail; black cloth fluttered in the wind. It was huge, much bigger than his raft. At least twenty-five feet long. Human figures were lined up along the deck, motionless. They were too far away for him to make out details.

Woody flattened his ears and growled. Terry shivered again. This time, it had nothing to do with the cold or dampness. He and Woody had been through a lot together. He'd learned to trust the dog's instincts about people.

The boat drew closer. Woody growled again, backing away from the edge of the raft. Terry did the same.

"Come on, Woody."

He whistled and the dog followed him. They ducked back inside their sleeping quarters. Woody shook himself again, splattering their cots with water. Terry barely noticed. He grabbed his old rifle and loaded it, making sure it was dry. He stuck extra rounds in his shirt pocket. Then he closed the door behind him and returned to the deck. Woody barked inside the toilet, upset at being left behind. He scratched at the door and whined.

"Stay," Terry said. "Until we find out what's going on."

The boat pulled alongside. The motor sputtered and then died. Eight people stared at him. There were five men and three women. All looked dirty and haggard. They were skinny;

their clothes hung from their frames like rags. Each of them was armed, some with rifles and others with baseball bats and lengths of pipe. Terry hefted the rifle, making sure they could see it but also trying to appear casual and non-threatening.

"Hello," one of the men called. His voice was sullen and tired. "Nice day."

Terry glanced up at the sky, and then back at the man. He blinked in confusion.

"It's a joke." The man laughed, revealing rotting teeth. "Gets 'em every time."

"Where you folks from?" Terry asked.

"All over. San Francisco, most of us. Occidental. Napa. We got a sick kid down below that says she's from Mount Shasta."

"What's wrong with her?"

"Don't know. Got some kind of white fungus growing up her arm. Picked her up yesterday, clinging to a grain silo. She's real sick. Wondered if you might have some medicine to trade?"

Terry frowned. He did have several bottles of ibuprofen and aspirin, as well as hydrogen peroxide and other things. But supplies were scarce and he wasn't keen on giving them up. Besides, he didn't have any fungicide.

"Not really," he apologized. "Sorry. But I would be willing to trade. I've got books. Stuff like that."

One of the other men scowled. "Books. The fuck we want with them?"

"Shut up, Beckham," the first man snapped. "I'm handling negotiations."

Frowning, Beckham fell silent.

"Don't have much need for books," the man said. "Except for maybe toilet paper. Got anything else?"

Terry shrugged. "What are you offering?"

"Half an hour with any of these fine ladies."

Terry flinched.

"Or Beckham, if he's more your taste."

"Hey," Beckham shouted, shoving the other man. "That shit ain't funny."

56

The other man winked at Terry. "How about it?"

"No," Terry stammered. "Neither. That's...no thank you."

He gripped the rifle tighter. Rain trickled down his forehead and into his eyes. The group on the boat appeared offended. Terry wondered how he could fix things. Before he could speak, Woody barked again. Everyone on the boat instantly became alert, leaning forward and clutching their weapons.

"You got a dog onboard?"

Terry nodded.

The man grinned. "Well hell, son—why didn't you say so. Books...that was pretty funny. How much you want for the dog?"

"Ought to see it first," another man muttered. "If it's skinny, won't be more than a mouthful."

"God damn it, Karnes, I'm talking here. You and Beckham keep your mouths shut." He turned back to Terry and smiled. "Look, I know what you're thinking. But we ain't pirates or nothing. We're just hungry. Food's scarce. Lost all our fishing tackle. Been living on seagulls and whatever we find floating in the water. Fresh meat would be real good. Seriously, friend, how much for the dog?"

"He's..."

"We've got ammo," the man interrupted. "Rounds for that .30-30. We got gasoline. Porno magazines. Batteries. Cases of bottled water. Rope. Whatever you want."

"The dog's not for sale," Terry said.

The man squinted. "Then we'll do this the hard way."

The rain fell harder.

Terry moved quickly, surprising even himself. He wasn't a spring chicken anymore, and between forced rationing and the weather, Terry wasn't in the best shape. But the threat against Woody galvanized him. He snapped the rifle up, set the stock against his shoulder, and squeezed off a shot before the others could even move. The leader toppled backward, a look of stunned disbelief on his face. Blood poured from his chest.

Terry worked the bolt and fired a second shot, sheering away the side of Karnes's face. Beckham and the women, armed only with bats and pipes, ducked below decks. The last man standing, armed with a pistol, fired back. Staying low, Terry exchanged gunfire with him. The man ducked behind a drum of rainwater.

"Wait," Terry shouted. "End this now and I'll let you guys leave unharmed."

"You shot Earl in the chest," the man yelled. "He's whistling through the bullet hole!"

"Put down your weapon and you can leave. Maybe save his life."

"You swear you'll let us go?"

"I promise."

The man crawled out from behind the barrel with his hands held high.

Terry shot him in the head.

Then he boarded the vessel and hunted down the rest, one by one. Food was scarce, after all. He didn't butcher the girl with the weird fungus growing on her, though. Instead, he threw her corpse over the side. Later, after he'd moved his belongings onto the boat, Terry and Woody lay back in their new bunks and listened to the waves.

"Yes indeed," he said, scratching Woody behind the ears. "This is the life. Nice, dry beds and plenty to eat."

He raised a warm can of Fosters and toasted their new home as they drifted into the night.

THE FIRST PRINCIPLE

"It's like God's pissing on us."

Mark Sylva grinned. "So the rain's a wicked pissah?"

"What?" O'Neill frowned.

"Pisser," Mark said, switching from his native Boston tongue to his more recently adopted Ohio accent.

Wilson cleared his throat. "Since both Mr. O'Neill and I are from out of town, we're fortunate that you're bilingual, Mr. Sylva. We'd be lost without your translations."

Mark blinked the rain from his eyes. Water dripped from the brim of his Red Sox cap, and his glasses kept fogging, making it hard for him to splice the wires.

"Old habits die hard," he said. "I lost some of my accent after moving to Ohio, but I fall back into it pretty easy every time I visit Bahstin."

While they laughed at his exaggerated pronunciation, Mark focused on rigging up a way to broadcast their distress signal. The three men stood atop the Prudential Building. Once, it had towered almost eight hundred feet above the city's skyline. Now, all but the top four floors were submerged beneath the Atlantic Ocean. The only other visible island was the John Hancock Tower. Everything else, including Mark's beloved Fenway Park, was at the bottom of the sea. So far, they hadn't spotted any survivors on the Hancock Tower's roof.

Mark knelt beneath the Pru's two-hundred foot radio tower. As a kid, he'd always thought the top of the Prudential Building looked like a ship. The array of radio antennas reminded him of masts. Now, here he was as an adult— onboard the ship he'd always thought it resembled. Him and the other castaways.

There were six of them left—Mark, O'Neill, Wilson, and the three Boston natives: Mason, Rebecca, and Herndon. The latter had been the Prudential Building's maintenance manager, and his knowledge of the structure had come in handy when Mark got the idea to record the distress signal. O'Neill was from Indiana, visiting Boston for a conference. Wilson was from Charleston, in town to deliver a speech. Both men were stranded in the city after the government-imposed travel restrictions due to the havoc created by the storms—and what came with the rain.

The same thing had happened to Mark. He'd been in town to visit old friends. His wife, Lisa, and two-year old son, Alexander, stayed home in Ohio. He didn't know where they were now. He liked to imagine that they might somehow hear his broadcast and know that he loved them and was still alive—if indeed he got it to work. If not, there was still the journal. When Alexander was born, Mark began keeping a journal for him. It had a leather cover and was written in pencil, so the ink wouldn't smear no matter how wet it got. Mark kept a log of Alex's accomplishments and how he felt about them. In addition to containing pictures and his son's first lock of hair, Mark had also written down wisdom and advice. That way, if something ever happened to him...

Mark still wrote in the journal every night.

There had been more survivors at first, but over time, they'd succumbed to illness and injury. Except for Norris, who'd been killed by something that resembled a human shark. Growing up, Mark had always wanted to be a marine biologist. He loved the ocean, spent hours in the tide pools searching for crabs, clams, and sea horses. Read dozens of books on marine biology and memorized the names of every fish he could. But he'd never seen anything like the monster that bit Norris in half.

Shuddering, Mark returned his attention to the electrical box.

"You sure this is gonna work?" O'Neill asked.

"It should," Mark said. "We've got plenty of diesel for the generator. I can broadcast just like a radio station. With all these radio masts and dishes, anyone with a working radio or television should hear it. Maybe even a CB radio. Television signals will only carry in the Massachusetts area, but the radio signals should hit tower after tower. They could go pretty far."

Maybe all the way to Ohio, he thought.

"And," he continued, "if I can figure out how to rewire the satellite dishes into the public broadcast system equipment, and the satellites out in space are still operational, I can transmit even farther."

"What if someone responds?" Wilson shivered beneath his umbrella.

Mark sighed. "I can only transmit. We won't know if anyone hears us unless a helicopter shows up to haul our asses out of here." He handed a pair of needle-nose pliers to O'Neill. "Hold those for me?"

Mark's shirtsleeve stretched as he handed O'Neill the tool, revealing his forearm.

"That's an interesting tattoo," Wilson observed.

"I've got a bunch. Chinese dragon on my leg. A tribal fire design with the Chinese symbol for a phoenix. A Celtic knot band around my upper arm, and the Chi symbol."

"Spiritual energy," Wilson said.

"Yeah!" Mark was surprised the old man knew what Chi meant. "And then I've got The Crow—you know, the comic book character? And a shark jaw with Tolkien runes of good and evil. Inside that is a symbol for balance and harmony."

"You are a very esoteric individual. I suppose you are well read?"

Mark nodded. "I think so."

"Are you familiar with Thales, the pre-Socratic Greek philosopher?"

"No," Mark admitted. "Don't think I ever Googled him."

Wilson grinned. "Thales proposed the foundational principles of existence—a cosmological doctrine. He believed that the world originated from water. Indeed, the universe was nothing more than a giant ocean that he referred to as the Great Deep. Earth formed by solidifying from the water on which it floated. One day, it would return to such. Thales called this the First Principle."

Mark glanced out at the ocean. "He thought the whole

planet was gonna turn into water?"

"Yes."

"Sounds to me like he wasn't that far off."

"Indeed."

A low, mournful howl echoed across the water. It sounded like a whale call—if the whale was part wolf. All three men jumped at the sound. O'Neill dropped the pliers into a puddle.

"Never get used to that," he muttered. "Damned things."

"One of the first laws of physics," Wilson continued after the cry had faded, "is that matter can neither be created nor destroyed. It can only change form. So, all this extra water around us has to be accounted for from the existing matter on the planet."

Mark fished the pliers out of the puddle. "What are you suggesting?"

"Perhaps the Earth itself is turning into liquid. That liquid is then evaporated and subsequently falls back down. Maybe the water around us isn't getting higher, but the ground is actually liquefying."

Mark frowned. "Earth is turning into a big water ball?"

"Possibly."

"So if the planet turns into water," O'Neill asked, "what keeps all that water from floating out into space?"

"Well," Wilson said, "the earth still has a core and is still rotating on its axis. That produces enough centrifugal force to maintain gravity. Plus, if only solid matter is being turned into water, the atmosphere won't be degraded. Think of it like a snow globe, or better yet, a bucket of water. If you put it on its side the water rushes out. If you spin it, the bucket can stay on its side and the water remains inside because of the force. The big question here is, what happens when the degradation hits the core?"

"Unless we freeze solid first," Mark said. "Winter's coming, after all."

"I don't think that will happen. If my theory is correct, all of that transforming matter is generating heat, raising the earth's temperature. Plus, it churns up warm water, the very kind necessary for the creation of hurricanes. That would explain all of the super storms we saw across the globe."

The pliers slipped in Mark's wet grasp, cutting his hand. Wincing, he sucked blood.

"It might explain the weather," he said. "But it doesn't explain those fucking things out there in the water."

"No," Wilson admitted. "I suppose it doesn't. I have no theory for the changes in our marine life."

"I do," O'Neill said. "Black magic."

"There's no such thing," Wilson scoffed.

"There was no such thing as half-human sharks, either," Mark said. "Until that one killed Norris."

Thunder rolled across the sky.

"You guys should get inside," Mark said. "Looks like more of that weird lightning is on the way. No sense in all three of us getting electrocuted."

"You sure?" O'Neill asked.

"Yeah, go on in. Grab something to eat. I'll be okay."

"No, I meant are you sure this thing will work."

Mark nodded. "It has to."

"Why?"

"Because people have always said I was lucky or blessed." Mark smiled. "Good things seem to happen to me. Why would that change now?"

After a moment, O'Neill returned his smile.

Wilson turned towards the stairwell. "We'll check on Mason and Rebecca—see if they are feeling better."

In the last few days, both Mason and Rebecca had contracted a fungal infection. Whitish fuzz sprouted on their extremities. Removing it had no effect. The substance just grew back. Both castaways were weak and thirsty.

After Wilson and O'Neill were gone, Mark finished his wiring. Then he retreated to the maintenance shed and shut the door behind him. He dried off with some shop rags and stripped down to his boxers. He hung his wet clothes up to dry. Then he put on his one spare pair of dry clothes. Finally, he powered up the generator and crossed his fingers.

Mark had grown up Catholic, just like the rest of Massachusetts. As an adult, his faith had faltered. But now he prayed.

"Please. Please let this work."

He keyed the microphone and looked at the transmitter, both of which were perched precariously on a card table. The transmitter's needle bobbed into the red. Mark cheered.

"Fifteen years as a telephone technician, baby!"

Grinning, Mark took a deep breath. He didn't know who was listening, but he didn't want to sound like an idiot in any case. He sat down behind the small card table and pulled the microphone closer. While he collected his thoughts, his ankle began to itch. Mark scratched it, but that only made the irritation worse.

"Probably just the dampness," he muttered. "Should go away soon enough. I just put on dry clothes."

He exhaled, pulled the microphone closer, and began to speak into it.

"My name is Mark Sylva. I'm coming to you live—that's right, still alive—from the roof of the Pru' Building in lovely, downtown Bahstin."

The itching on his ankle grew worse. Mark scratched it vigorously. His fingernails drew blood.

"Please stand-by. We're already experiencing technical difficulties."

Cringing, he let go of the mike and rolled up his pants leg. Then he pulled down his sock. Fungus—the same as on Mason and Rebecca—was growing on his ankle; the spot was about the size of a half-dollar. Mark turned his attention back to the radio.

"The first thing I want to say is this—Lisa and Alex, I love you."

He scratched again.

"Anyway, here I am. Hope somebody is listening. I always figured that when I died, I'd go out with a fight, getting back up to attack one more time, like Boromir in Lord of the Rings or Willem Dafoe in Platoon. I'm a sucker for those great last stands. But lately, I've been wondering. A friend of mine just told me about the First Principle. Maybe we should talk about that."

The itching grew worse. The fuzz spread.

"Damn," Mark said. "I'm really thirsty."

IN THE SHADOW
OF TARANAKI

Hawera, New Zealand

The Maori had a saying about Mount Egmont (or Mount Taranaki, as it was called in the Maori tongue): "If you can see the mountain it's going to rain. If you can't see it, then it's already raining."

Mean considered this as he trudged through the downpour, and tried not to laugh. He was afraid that if he started laughing, he might not be able to stop.

The dormant volcano had always loomed over Hawera, dominating the horizon. But the Maori had been right. Since the rains began, the mountain had been shrouded in mist and no longer visible. But it was still there. It had to be. Because if it wasn't, then Mean was fucked.

And in truth, he was probably fucked anyway.

Hawera was a sleepy little town, and its ten-thousand residents didn't worry about much. When the global mega-storms started, the townspeople watched it all on television, annoyed that the coverage preempted their rugby matches. Mean had just returned from a trip to the U.K.—attending a comic book convention in Birmingham—and was grateful to be home and away from all that adolescent body odor. But soon, he wished he was back in England, or anywhere else for that matter. Hawera had numerous streams, lakes and ponds, and was close to the sea. All of this combined into a recipe for disaster. Powerful storm surges took out Waihi beach and then rushed inland, smashing over the towering cliffs and eroding the countryside. At the same time, the rain-swollen streams and ponds overflowed their banks, flooding the town and surrounding communities. The deluge wiped out Hawera within hours. Those not killed in the flash flooding had evacuated to Ohawe, nearly nine kilometers away. Then came word that Ohawe was gone, too.

That was when Mean decided to head for Mount Egmont. He went alone, armed with his .22 semi-auto and a backpack filled with medicine, water and canned goods. He wrapped a plastic bag around the backpack to keep its contents dry. The muddy terrain sucked at his boots. Trees and other vegetation were starting to collapse, their roots unable to keep purchase in the wet soil. At times, the water reached his knees. Mean wasn't worried. He could swim. If things got worse, he could build a raft. He'd grown up on a farm, breeding racehorses. It had a stream out back; the Maori name for the stream was long and unpronounceable. Mean and his friends had always referred to it as "The River." As a kid, he'd spent many hours floating down the stream with rafts made from oil drums and a few planks tied together with baling twine.

He got a lump in his throat at the memory. The stream was gone now, like the rest of the waterways in the region—all part of something much bigger.

Mean pulled his coat tighter around himself and continued on his way, following a steep goat track that wound up between the cliffs. His feet were cold and wet, and night was coming. There wasn't really daylight anymore. There was only varying shades of grey. With no lights or stars for illumination, nighttime was pitch black now. Primordial. He'd have to find shelter soon, here in the foothills at the base of the mountain, and continue his ascent tomorrow. If he fumbled around in the dark, he could fall off a cliff. And if he didn't get dry and warm soon, he was sure to catch hypothermia.

Through the swirling fog, he spotted a cave ahead, and made for it. The opening was a narrow fissure, leading downward at a sharp angle. Water trickled into the opening. Mean unslung his backpack, ducked his head, and crept inside. After a few feet, the tunnel straightened. The water pooled on the floor. Mean pressed onward, until he found a dry section. He rummaged through the backpack, found his flashlight, and surveyed the interior. It was perfect. He was alone, and more importantly, dry.

Sitting with his back against the cave wall, Mean closed his eyes and sighed.

His eyes snapped open when he heard the shrieks. They didn't sound human. After a brief moment, he recognized them. As a boy, Mean had shot rabbits with an old single-action .22 rifle. He'd never forget the sound the rabbits made when wounded. They screamed. The sound had sent shivers down his spine. That was what he heard now.

Curious, Mean crept to the cave entrance, carrying his flashlight and the gun. When he got outside, the screams grew louder, echoing over the constant drum of the falling rain.

A mass exodus of animals charged out of the undergrowth and scampered up the mountain. He saw rabbits, flightless kiwi birds, kiore rats, deer, wild goats and pigs, and even a runaway cow. Birds and pekapeka bats fluttered overhead. Mean wondered what had disturbed them all. They were obviously distressed, ignoring each other as well as the human in their midst, in an effort to flee. Deep within the mist, he heard a squelching sound.

Then the predator—the cause of the wildlife's fright—slithered forth, driving another wave of panicked animals before it. It was a giant worm, roughly the size of a small compact car, and of undetermined length. The monster's tail-end was still shrouded in mist. As Mean gaped, it surged forth and swallowed a rabbit whole. It never slowed, targeting the next morsel as it wriggled through the mud. Amazingly, smaller worms clung to its hide—New Zealand flatworms, normally found on South Island. Carnivorous and predatory, they fed on other worms by lying on top of them and excreting acidic digestive juices. Then they sucked up the soup. Apparently, their presence had little effect on the bigger worm.

Mean raised the .22 and took aim. His hands and legs felt numb, and his ears rang.

Shock, he thought. *I'm going into shock.*

He was about to squeeze the trigger when something brown and furry leaped ahead of the worm and ran towards him. Mean had time to register that it was an opossum. Then the animal climbed up his leg like it was a tree trunk and wrapped itself around his head. Mean let out a muffled scream as the terrified opossum roped its prehensile tail around his neck and dug into his scalp with its long, sharp claws. The thing was incredibly strong. Mean yelled, beating at it with his flashlight. The opossum clung tighter. The pain was intense and the smell from its wet fur was revolting.

Unable to see, Mean heard the giant worm slithering closer. He ran blind, stumbling over the rocks and almost slipping in the mud. He dropped the flashlight and the gun and gripped the animal with both hands. Pulling with all his might, Mean yanked the creature free. Its claws left deep, ragged gashes in his scalp and face. It wriggled in his grip, tail lashing the air like a whip.

"Get off me," he shouted.

The opossum squealed. Mean smashed it against a boulder, hearing the bones snap. Seizing it by the tail, he swung the creature over his head and slammed it repeatedly against the stone. Then he flung it to the ground and stomped on it until it was a red, jellied pulp. His boots were covered in gore. Blood flecked his face—both his and the opossum's.

Behind him, the worm slithered closer. Mean glanced around for the gun, but it was missing, swallowed up by the marshy terrain. As the worm closed the distance between them, he turned and ran, fleeing along with the rest of the animal procession, into the shadows of Mount Taranaki. The worm undulated after them all, single-mindedly determined.

More animals screamed in the darkness. Mean screamed louder.

RIDING THE STORM OUT

Modesto, California

"Water, water everywhere, and not a drop to drink…"

Larry Roberts licked his cracked, bleeding lips and tried to remember what the line was from. Some story about a mariner? He should know. Books were his life. He read them. Sold them. What was it from? He didn't know anymore. What he did know was that he was suffering from dehydration. He was on part of a roof that had been torn from a house. Surrounded by water, floating on water, water falling from the fucking sky—and yet he was slowly dying of thirst. His mouth was dry and felt like cotton. There were no tears when he cried. He pissed once a day now—if that—and his urine was brown. Larry felt lightheaded most of the time. His skin was cool to the touch, his heartbeat rapid. And now he couldn't think, either.

A corpse bumped into his makeshift raft. The slight impact made the roof bob up and down. The body rolled over as it floated past. Something had eaten its face.

Larry huddled beneath a canvas tarp, shivering and soaked. This was all he had—a roof and a tarp. No food. No dry clothes. No matches or weapons. His last meal had been two days ago—a pigeon he'd killed with his bare hands. He ate it raw, gagging with every bite, but chewing ravenously.

The water around him was unfit for human consumption and full of Modesto's remains—dead bodies and chemicals and debris. The stench made him nauseous. He couldn't drink the rain, either. He had no way to catch it, other than cupping his hands. The drops felt oily. Slimy. And before riding the storm out on this roof, Larry had heard from other survivors that the rain was poison. If you drank it, you got infected with some kind of fungus—a whitish mold that eventually covered your entire body. That was the rumor, at least.

Larry believed it. Three days ago, he'd seen a man clinging to the top of a tree jutting from the water. Well, not a man, but a man-shaped thing. A figure composed of white fuzz that waved its arms and moaned when it saw him. The creature had slipped into the water as Larry neared it. He'd panicked, waiting for it to surface on the roof, but the tide carried him away before the thing emerged.

Drinking the water was suicide. But he was so thirsty. He listened to the rain as it drummed against the tiles, and tried to remember his family's names—and found that he couldn't anymore. Larry looked up at the stormy sky and wished that he could weep.

Then he saw a light—a strange red glow flashing behind the black, roiling clouds. As he watched, the clouds parted and a phantom ship sailed out of the breach, floating far above the sea. It was an old vessel, and appeared to be damaged. There was a jagged hole in the side. One of the masts had been snapped off and the tattered sails fluttered in the wind. Despite the damage, it flew.

Hovered.

Whatever.

"I'm in worse shape than I thought."

His voice was hoarse and weak. Larry felt like laughing, but he was afraid that if he started, he might not be able to stop.

The ship slowed. A rope ladder plummeted from the deck and hung directly overhead. Arms and legs trembling, Larry grasped the rope and tried to climb. He felt a twinge of unease as his feet left the roof. He glanced up at the flying ship, but couldn't see anybody onboard. He climbed higher, not looking down. His weakness grew. Larry clung to the rope, unable to proceed. He squeezed his eyes shut and gasped for breath. Suddenly, the ladder began to rise on its own. Somebody was pulling him up. He kept his eyes closed.

Eventually, Larry felt rough hands grasping him. He opened his eyes and saw a dozen men pulling him over the rail and onto the deck.

"Easy, lad," one of them said. "We've got you."

The men smelled like road kill. They sat him down on the wet deck. Blinking, Larry studied his rescuers. They were dressed in the tattered remains of antique costumes, and armed with rusty muskets and cutlasses—rejects from a Pirates of the Caribbean movie. The largest, a rotund man with a wiry, unkempt beard, stepped forward.

"Welcome aboard, mate. I'm Captain Hendrik van der Decken."

Larry stumbled to his feet. His head swam and he lost his balance. Hands reached out to support him.

"W-where am I?" Larry mumbled. "What's happening?"

"You are onboard the Flying Dutchman," the Captain said. "We sailed from Amsterdam in 1641, in the employ of the Dutch East India Company. After a highly successful trip to the Far East, we were on our way back to Holland. As we approached the tip of Africa, in the Cape of Good Hope, a storm came up. Not like the storm that covers the globe now, but a bad one nonetheless. The wind was against us and we made no headway. I commanded my men to lay on steady. The storm wouldn't stop us. I swore we'd continue sailing. Told my first mate, 'May I be eternally damned if I head for shore, though I should beat about here till the day of judgment.' The Lord must have taken offense at my blasphemy because here we are. We have sailed around the world, unable to die or put in to shore. We've no provisions, yet we need not eat."

"So you're ghosts?"

"No. We are not dead, but neither are we alive. We are cursed to roam, just like Cain and the Wandering Jew." The Captain swept his hand towards the rail, gesturing at the rain. "But now our long cruise is nearly over, for surely this is Judgment Day. Soon, we shall make our final port of call… and rest."

Larry nodded in agreement. They were right; this was the end of the world. He cleared his throat and tried to work up enough saliva to speak.

"Thanks for rescuing me," he said. "I thought for sure I was a dead man."

"Not yet, lad. You can ride the storm with us."

Larry glanced over the rail. Below him, the waters over Modesto soared by as the ship picked up speed again. He became aware of how close the crew stood, encircling him.

"Please," Larry croaked. "Do you have any water? Wine? Anything? I'm really thirsty."

The Captain's expression was sad. "And so you will be for as long as you remain aboard. As I said, we are not dead, but neither are we alive. You are not the first castaway we've picked up. As long as you stay onboard the Flying Dutchman, you remain perpetually frozen in time. Harkon, there, had a broken leg when the storm came upon us. It has remained broken all these centuries. I'm afraid you will remain thirsty until we are finally free of the curse."

"Shit."

The Captain stepped closer, his hand encircling the cutlass at his side. "Of course, with your throat cut, your thirst won't matter."

"What?"

The crew seized him again. Larry struggled, but in his weakened state, his efforts were futile. They held his arms and grabbed his hair, jerking his head back. The Captain eyed his throat.

"We have no need of food, but neither are we content to accept our fate. We've spit in God's eye since the curse began. At first, it was to insult him. But eventually, we found that we liked the abominations we enacted."

"What are you going to do with me?"

"Put you in the hold, along with the rest of the castaways we've picked up throughout the years. We'll slice your throat every night and fill our goblets with your blood. And since you cannot die, we'll do the same the next night, and every night throughout eternity."

Larry turned pale.

"Be glad you are not a woman. We do other things to them, aye?"

"Y-you're insane! Let me go!"

The Captain laughed. "Hear that, lads? He thinks we are insane."

The sailors laughed.

"We are insane," the Captain growled. "As you would be, if you shared our fate for as long as we have. But with Judgment Day nigh, perhaps you will not suffer as long as the rest of our guests."

Larry squirmed. "Let go of me, you bastards!"

"Take him below," the Captain ordered.

With all of his remaining strength, Larry tore free of his captors and ran for the rail. Crying out, they charged after him. Larry slammed into the rail and toppled over it. As he plummeted, he refused to scream.

It took him a long time to reach the ocean. The rain lashed at him and the wind whistled in his ears. When the fall was over, Larry wasn't thirsty anymore.

BAD FISH

Somewhere in the New Atlantic

Brian Lee was sick of fish. Since leaving home on his twenty-seven-foot Baja 272, all he'd had to eat were fish and one molting seagull. Since there was no way to cook them, he'd eaten both the bird and the fishes raw—something that got easier every time. The bird had been the worst—chewy and cold and full of gristle. Worse, its lower half had some kind of weird fungus growing on it. He'd been careful not to eat that part, but devoured the rest, guts and all, and then puked when he was done. But that had been weeks ago, and Brian had eaten so many fish since then that a fresh seagull now would be fine dining.

He turned his head to the sky. Raindrops blinded him, streaming down his upturned face. Brian held his pants up with one hand. His wet T-shirt, which had been tight-fitting before the rains started, now hung loose.

"Let it rain cookies," he shouted. "Let it rain potato chips or pizza or popcorn. Or a steak. Anything!"

The storm clouds didn't answer. He hadn't expected them to. Even though he was alone, Brian spoke aloud every day. He was afraid that if he didn't, he might forget how. He was very lonely. Worse, he was afraid he might be going mad. At night, he sometimes heard voices singing over the roaring waves. They belonged to his wife, Theresa, and his daughters, Kirsten, Jessica, and Kimberly. Of course, that was impossible. His family was gone. But each time he heard those phantom songs, Brian had to restrain himself from jumping overboard, convinced Theresa and the kids were floating somewhere nearby—perhaps swimming like they did in their backyard pool back home in Goffstown. After a few nights of that, Brian

74

had started stuffing his ears with strips of cloth and tying his legs to the bed when he slept.

Thoughts of his family and their home made him think of Goffstown. Would he ever see it again? Doubtful. Goffstown, like the rest of New Hampshire, was underwater now.

Brian's Baja 272 had been docked on the shore of Lake Winnipesauke, along with their Honda wave runner. They hadn't used either one very much, which was a shame. Boating on Lake Winn could be an adventure, with all of the rocks, islands, and stupid people. It hadn't been until Lake Winn was swallowed up by the Atlantic that he finally got to use the boat. In the weeks since, when he grew tired of eating raw fish and the loneliness and the boredom and the rain—especially the rain—Brian occasionally thought of just slipping overboard and swimming away until he drowned. It wasn't a rational or sane impulse, but he had it just the same.

He could swim, but not well. His problem was simple— he sunk. He couldn't tread water because he tired out quickly. When he'd been fifteen, Brian had gone to Boy Scout camp, and had to take a swim test. He was required to jump in the lake and swim one hundred yards in order to pass and receive his badge. He jumped in and nearly died of shock. It was late July, but the water was absolutely frigid. Brian did three laps and got out, shivering and completely drained. He crawled back to his tent and threw up. The scoutmaster took pity on him and gave him a badge anyway.

He was thinking about this and ignoring the gnawing pains in his stomach when he saw the seagulls. His mouth watered as he watched them swoop overhead. They dived down to the surface, scooped debris from the water, and then soared back into the sky. A few of them were daring enough to land on his boat, desperate for a place to rest. Poor things looked exhausted. Brian didn't care. They were dinner.

He edged towards the closest bird, careful not to scare it. The seagull cocked its head and stared at him, unblinking. Something splashed out in the water, but Brian ignored it. It wasn't until the rest of the seagulls began shrieking that he turned his attention back to the sea.

A school of silver fish shot out of the water and into the sky. Each was about eight inches long. Their eyes were large and bulbous, and their pectoral fins were broad and curved like wings. In fact, they were wings. Brian had heard of flying fish, of course, but he'd never seen them before. He forgot all about the birds and watched the fish, delighted at their aerial acrobatics. More of them burst from the waves. They swam just below the surface, with their fins tucked close to their bodies. Then, as they left the water, they spread their fins and glided through the air. Laughing, Brian grinned. The seagulls squawked with delight and dived down to meet this flying smorgasbord. Birds and fish crashed together. Brian's laughter faded. Then he screamed.

The fish had teeth. Like flying piranhas, they ripped through the seagulls, shredding and tearing. Blood and feathers joined the rain falling from the sky. Then came severed bird heads, feet and beaks. The surviving seagulls scattered, trying to flee, but the fish turned in mid-air and circled around for another attack.

Brian threw up his hands as more blood and feathers plummeted towards him. The rain's pace seemed to increase with the slaughter. It fell quicker, drumming against the deck. There were more splashes from all around the boat as school after school of carnivorous fish leapt from the water and joined the hunt. Their silver bodies flashed in the gloom. Then they glided towards the boat.

Panicked, Brian ran across the wet deck, one hand gripping the rail to keep from slipping. His heart pounded in his throat. He was dimly aware that he was crying and screaming at the same time. He shouted for Theresa and the girls. Their songs were silent now, if they'd ever actually existed at all. The only sound was the drone of his pursuers. Their wing-fins hummed slightly. The noise from their gnashing teeth swelled, drowning out everything else.

He glanced from side to side. There was nowhere to hide. He was defenseless. Weaponless. In seconds, they'd be on him, stripping him to the bone. Brian's shoulders slumped. He hung his head. There was only one way out—the ocean.

If he ducked below the surface long enough, maybe the fish would forget about him and move on. All he had to do was avoid sinking. This was the biggest Boy Scout merit badge of his life.

With a final anguished cry, Brian vaulted over the side of the boat. The fish swarmed him as he plunged towards the water, and what sank beneath the surface was red, wet and ragged.

LOADS AND LOADS

Worcester, England

When the looters arrived, Stephen "Macker" McDornell and his three year-old son, Charlie, hid inside a toilet stall. Stephen made a game out of it and told Charlie to stay quiet. He did. Charlie was a good boy.

For the last several days, they'd been holed up in the football stadium, famous for being the highest league ground in England—one hundred and sixty-eight meters above sea level. The league ground and the steeple of the cathedral that had once overlooked the River Severn were all that remained above water now. Everything else had been swallowed by the sea. The river. The rain. Whatever. They were all the same now. They were all water.

Before the current disaster, the worst flooding Stephen had ever seen was last summer when the river breached its banks, damaging thousands of homes and submerging whole villages along its banks underwater. But this...this was far worse. Worcester was gone. Not flooded, but gone. Vanished beneath the waves. And even though Stephen secretly considered that an improvement, it was still heart wrenching—not so much that Worcester was destroyed, but all the people that had been destroyed along with it. His mates and Wendy (Stephen's former girlfriend and Charlie's mum), and even his co-workers at the firm where he'd worked as a printer (although he didn't miss them that much). It was hard to believe that he'd never drink a pint with his friends again, or root alongside them for West Brom. God...West Brom! Hard to fathom that there would be no more matches. Stephen had been a season ticket holder for all home league games. They'd been doing so well after missing out on promotion last season by one bloody goal

78

in the very last game. Now, there would be no more games.

The hardest thing to accept, by far, was that Charlie would never see his mum again. The boy still asked for her at night. Stephen thought of her each day, while fighting for his and Charlie's survival. They'd recently split after being together for twelve years, but he still cared for her. He wished things were different now. The apocalypse had a way of making a man see what was important.

He cocked his head, listening. Outside was silence.

"My Mickey," Charlie whispered.

Stephen put a finger to his lips. "Where is it?" he mouthed.

Charlie shrugged, pouting. "I dropped it."

Stephen groaned. They'd fled in such a hurry that he hadn't noticed his son had dropped his favorite toy—a stuffed Mickey Mouse that Charlie took everywhere. He loved it more than SpongeBob SquarePants or Homer Simpson. The boy couldn't sleep without his Mickey. If it was gone for good, that would be very bad. It was irreplaceable.

"Stay here," Stephen told him.

He crept to the restroom's door and listened. He heard voices beyond, and strained to hear them.

"Somebody's been here. But they're gone now."

"Are you sure?"

"Sure, we're sure. We checked everywhere, didn't we?"

"Bollocks."

Two speakers, both male. Stephen continued eavesdropping. It was difficult to hear over the rain.

"Are we going to stay, then?"

"Don't see that we have a choice, what with the boat springing a leak. If you find anyone, kill them. This is our home now."

Stephen flinched. Any ideas he'd had of trying to negotiate withered. These were hard men, and he'd have to deal with them accordingly. He tiptoed back to the stall and pulled Charlie close.

"I'm going to go find your Mickey," he whispered. "But I need you to stay here and keep very, very quiet. Can you do that for Daddy?"

Charlie nodded.

"It's important. You have to pretend there are monsters outside, and you can't let them hear you."

Charlie's eyes got big. Stephen hated doing this to him, but there was no choice.

"Daddy?"

"What?"

"That's me." He tapped the tattoo on Stephen's forearm— an ambigram of Charlie's name.

Stephen tried to speak around the lump in his throat, and found he couldn't. He nodded, swallowing it down. Charlie was a fifth attempt at in vitro fertilization, and was born seven weeks premature. He'd spent the first fourteen days of his life in the hospital. Everyone said he was a Daddy's Boy. He held Stephen's hand wherever they went.

"How much do you love me?" Stephen asked, smiling.

Charlie answered the way he always did. He stretched his little arms out wide, made a face like he was taking a dump, and said, "Loads and loads."

"Stay here," Stephen whispered, getting to his feet. "And stay quiet. I'll be back soon."

Armed with a broken mop handle that he'd fashioned into a spear when they first arrived, Stephen crept outside. There was no sign of the looters. He carefully retraced his steps, and spied Mickey. The doll was lying in the mud and wet grass at the center of the league ground. Before he could go for it, he heard footsteps coming his way.

Stephen hid behind a row of seats. A disheveled man appeared, dressed in wet, soiled rags. He appeared sick. Thin strands of white fuzz sprouted from his fingers and face, and his eyes were red and rheumy. One hand clutched a very large knife. Stephen waited until he had passed by and then tiptoed out behind him. Gritting his teeth, he jabbed the spear forward, plunging it into the man's back. The man screamed, trying to turn around. The knife fell from his hand. Stephen pressed harder and the spear went all the way through. The man collapsed, sliding off the spear with a sucking sound.

"Chuck?" Another man's voice called out, but Stephen couldn't tell where the speaker was located.

Moving quickly, he bent over, picked up the knife, and slashed the intruder's throat. Then he ran for the ground, feet pounding against the cement, intent on leading the other looters away from Charlie. He heard shouts behind him. Stephen turned and saw two men pursuing him.

He reached the ground and ran out onto the field. The mud sucked at his shoes, and the rain pelted his body. The men behind him were faster. Stephen turned again and his eyes widened; they'd closed more than half the distance between them.

"Leave us alone," he hollered.

The men didn't respond. There was murder in their eyes.

Stephen reached Mickey and bent over to pick him up. As he stood again, the ground where the doll had been lying exploded, showering him with mud and grass. Something pale and grey—the size of a dog—thrust itself from the hole. Stephen screamed. It was a giant worm. Dripping slime, the creature wriggled forth. Stephen thrust his spear into its head. Brownish liquid gushed from the wound. The monster squirmed and twisted. Then Stephen turned and ran back towards his pursuers.

Their shrieks greeted him. Two more worms had emerged from the earth, seizing both men in their massive mouths. The creatures made no sound as they attacked. Inch by inch, the struggling looters disappeared down the worms' throats.

Still clutching Mickey, he made it back to the bleachers and glanced down at the field. The worms had burrowed back beneath the ground, but he was pretty sure they couldn't reach him up here. He made his way back to the loo, and heard Charlie sobbing quietly. When he entered the restroom, the boy ran to him and threw his arms around his father.

"What's all this?" Stephen asked, wiping his tears away.

"I heard shouting. Were they the monsters?"

"Yes," Stephen said, "but you don't have to worry now. The monsters are gone. And look what I found."

He held up Mickey. Squealing in delight, Charlie grabbed

the toy and held it tight.

"My Mickey! I love you, Daddy."

"I love you too, Charlie. Loads and loads."

Outside, the rain continued to fall, but neither one of them cared.

MESSAGE IN A BOTTLE

Columbus, Ohio

"I always figured that if I was going to bite the big one, I'd go out with a fight, like Willem Dafoe in Platoon. I'm a sucker for those great last stands. But now, I don't know. I doubt it will happen like that. This shit is spreading."

Mike Goffee nodded, agreeing with the voice on the radio. Of all the ways he could die, he'd never figured it would be a worldwide flood.

"Anyway," the man on the radio continued, "this is day two of my broadcast and nobody has shown up to rescue us yet. My name's Mark Sylva. If anybody is listening, we're on top of the Prudential Building in Boston. We're sick."

"You're better off than me," Mike told the radio. "At least you've got a roof over your head."

Mike and his two black cats, Midnight and Dusty, occupied a small, featureless island jutting up from the waters over Columbus. Before finding land, they'd drifted in an eight-foot long aluminum bass boat. Unable to swim and unfamiliar with boats, Mike had been grateful when their craft came to rest against the island. The outcropping was roughly twenty square feet, barely big enough for him and the cats, and devoid of buildings, trees or grass. With the ferocity of the storm and the rain hampering his visibility, Mike couldn't tell what it was. The gray surface was hard like rock, but smooth—no cracks or fissures. It was also slightly bulbous and had a small hill in the center. He'd tried to remember the city's geography, but couldn't place the island. Eventually, he'd assumed it was the top of a water tower or similar structure. Whatever the island's origin, it was better than drifting around in the boat.

The guy on the radio kept talking. "Boston is underwater,

83

except for us and another building. I keep thinking about my wife and son in Ohio. I just hope things are better there."

Mike looked out at the surrounding ocean and shook his head.

"Not really."

He turned the radio off to conserve the batteries. Then he put it inside a plastic bag and returned it to the footlocker, so it would stay dry. He only used it once a day, hoping to hear an official broadcast—news or a message from the authorities. Word that, unlike Hurricane Katrina, the government was on top of things this time. Instead, the airwaves were filled with static, interrupted occasionally by other survivors like the guy in Boston.

Midnight and Dusty were curled up in the corner of the makeshift shelter. They meowed at him. Mike felt sorry for the cats. They were wet and cold and hungry. Miserable, just like him. They'd actually seemed to grow more uneasy since landing on the island. Maybe the cats preferred boat life.

With no buildings or shelter on the island, Mike had flipped the boat over and propped up one end with two oars. Then he'd draped some canvas tarps and plastic sheeting over the sides. It didn't completely keep the water out, but it gave the three of them a semi-dry place to sleep and to store their belongings. It wasn't the sturdiest shelter in the world, but as long as they didn't bump the oars, it stayed upright.

With the radio stowed away, Mike slipped out of his wet boots, rung out his hat, and listened to the waves lap against the island. The water was full of dead people and debris, and Mike spent his days retrieving what he could. Anything that came within reach was fair game. He'd found very little food, but that was okay. They'd had supplies on the boat. Still, he'd rescued all sorts of useful items from the surf.

When he was semi-dry, Mike turned his attention to the day's plunder. The first thing he'd recovered today was a clear plastic bottle. He'd hoped it contained soda, or better yet, clean water. His heart sank when he saw that it didn't. The only thing inside was a piece of paper. Mike unscrewed the cap and pulled the paper out. He unfolded it.

It was a note, scrawled in what appeared to be a woman's handwriting, on lined tablet paper with ballpoint pen. Shivering in the damp, chilly air, Mike read it.

When things got bad, we left Cincinnati on Harley's yacht. Yes, I know, I know. I was planning on telling him about me and Dimitri. Planning on leaving him right after my birthday. But I didn't know the end of the world would happen first, did I? That's how we ended up together. Me, Harley, the kids— and Dimitri. My family and my lover. One big happy group. Of course, to Harley and the kids, Dimitri was just the gardener. We sailed around and Harley had to be in charge, of course.

We saw other people in boats, or clinging to wreckage and sitting on rooftops. Harley refused to help them. Said we couldn't take anyone else onboard. That we only had enough supplies for us. So we just left them there.

Harley insisted that we should head west. He said the farther we were from the waterways, the better off we'd be. Dimitri and I told him that didn't matter because the water was everywhere, but Harley didn't listen. We couldn't find any dry land. The rain got into everything. Our clothes, our supplies, the gas tank. Maybe even our heads. That must have been it. Why else would Harley have snapped the way he did? When he tried to throw Dimitri overboard, I hit him in the head with the fire extinguisher. I wasn't expecting the sound it made, or all that blood. So much blood. Too much. The kids were sleeping below decks when it happened. When they woke up, we told them that Daddy had fallen over the side in the night.

So much for that. Except that neither Dimitri or I knew how to pilot the boat. We just sort of drifted. Our supplies ran low.

Then we found an island. We couldn't see much of it, because of the rain, but when we got close enough to swim, we jumped off the yacht and made for it. Thank God I insisted on getting the kids swimming lessons last summer. Anyway, there wasn't much on the island. In fact, there wasn't anything. But it was solid, at least. But as we watched the boat drift away,

I told Dimitri we'd made the wrong decision. The island was small and there was nothing for us to take shelter under. We sat there and huddled up against each other. All we had was what was in our packs. A few bottles of water. Some canned vegetables. My tablet and pen and lighter and cell phone, all of which I'd stored in a plastic bag. And the stupid cell phone still wouldn't work. And we were hungry and wet and cold and then things got worse.

The island wasn't. It was...woke up. This thing moved. It came up out of the water so suddenly and the kids were screaming and they slid down the side and into its mouth and then they weren't screaming anymore and that was worse and then Dimitri and I were in the water and the thing was swimming away and it looked kind of like a cross between a dinosaur and a whale, but its colors were all wrong because we'd thought it was an island. And Dimitri was dead and his legs were gone below the knees but I floated on top of him and wrote this and please somebody come help me. Please, please PLEASE! I'm sorry for what I did. I don't want to die. It's coming back. The island is alive.

Mike finished reading and glanced down at the cats. Dusty purred at his side, despite her obvious discomfort. He rolled the paper back up and placed it in the footlocker. It would come in useful if he ever found matches or a cigarette lighter. Then he sat the empty bottle outside the boat, hoping to catch some rainwater so that their supply of bottled water would last longer.

Finished, Mike lay back beneath the boat and tried to get comfortable. It was impossible. With the footlocker and the cats, he barely had room to lie down, let alone stretch out. He thought about the note. Granted, the weather phenomena was weird, but this? The ramblings of a crazy person, obviously. There were probably a lot of people out there like that, trapped and alone and slowly going mad. The guy on the radio in Boston, talking about some weird fungal disease. The woman who'd written this note. When civilization collapsed, a lot of people's minds had collapsed with it.

Could be me, he thought, and then shrugged. At least he still had the cats. And food and water.

The ground trembled slightly. He felt the vibration run through him.

"What the—"

Midnight hissed. A moment later, Dusty growled, low and deep in her throat. Both cats scratched at the ground beneath them. Midnight was de-clawed but still pawed the surface with an intense urgency. Startled, Mike looked around.

"What's wrong?"

Their cries changed to frantic mewling. Both cats darted out from beneath the shelter and ran into the rain. Mike crawled out from beneath the boat and shouted for them. Then he felt the island shudder.

"Oh God..."

Beneath him, the island moved again.

His screams were lost beneath the island's roar.

THE MAGI

Burwood East, Victoria, Australia

There wasn't much to see. Black, dirty water. Floating debris. Dead things. It was like having a picture window overlooking hell.

Penny Khaw and Leigh Haig had taken shelter in the top of the Glen Waverly Police Academy chapel, about six kilometers from their home. Looking west, where the city of Melbourne used to be, they saw waves breaking against the top of the Eureka Tower and a few other tall buildings. To the east, the peaks of the Dandenong Mountains jutted from the water. Everything else was gone.

In the background, The Whitlams' "You Sound Like Louis Burdett" played softly on their battery-powered stereo. The sound of the rain almost drowned it out. They stood there, watching the water rise, and Penny tried not to cry. Her breath caught in her throat. She stiffened as Leigh put his arm around her shoulders and gently squeezed.

"We've got clean water," he said, "and food. And kerosene for the heater. We'll be fine."

"Food?" Penny's hands went to her swelling stomach. "We can't just live on double chocolate Tim Tams and jars of vegemite. We need real food."

"Tim Tams *are* real food."

Despite her fears, Penny smiled. Leigh leaned over and brushed her ear with his lips. She knew she shouldn't be so hard on him. He was just trying to focus on the positive—cheer her up. Sighing, she leaned into him and relaxed.

"Seriously," she whispered. "What are we going to do?"

"You're thirteen weeks today. There's plenty of time to plan. I'll take care of everything."

88

"But there are no doctors left. No hospitals. We don't even have clean clothes."

He hugged her tighter. "Let's not worry about that now. I'll handle it."

"You're going to deliver the baby?" Penny's tone was dubious.

"If I have to," Leigh insisted. "But that's months away. There's still time. First thing I'll do tomorrow is go scavenging. Maybe I'll even find other survivors. Maybe a midwife—or a nurse."

Penny heard the desperation in his voice and wondered if he believed his words or if he was just saying them for her benefit—and the baby's.

"How can you go for supplies? You can't swim."

"Sure I can. I may not be the greatest swimmer in style or speed, but I can make my way from point A to B if it's not too far. Anything over two kilometers would leave me pretty much screwed, but hopefully, I won't have to go that far. Maybe I can find a boat."

"What do you know about boating?"

"Didn't I ever tell you? My Dad was in the Victorian Water Police for over twenty-five years. I spent some time when I was younger out on the police boats. I picked up some boating knowledge; I certainly have enough to get around out there."

"But you're forgetting one thing."

Leigh frowned. "What's that?"

"Everything is underwater. There's nothing to salvage. No one to find. We're all that's left, Leigh. It's just the three of us."

He didn't answer. At first, Penny worried that she'd offended him somehow. But then she realized that he was staring out at the water.

"I think," Leigh whispered, "that you might be wrong about that."

He pointed. Penny peered through the heavy downpour. Then she gasped.

"A boat..."

Leigh's voice rose in excitement. "See that? We're rescued!"

"Maybe," she agreed. "But they might not even know we're here. We should call out—signal them somehow."

"No need. Look, they're heading straight toward us."

The boat shot across the water, bouncing up and down on the waves, propelled by a loud outboard motor. The craft bore down on the chapel. As it drew nearer, they saw three figures onboard, dressed in drab green ponchos, rain-slicked and weather-beaten. At least one of them was armed with a rifle.

Penny felt a sudden flash of unease. "Should we hide?"

Leigh shrugged. "Maybe you should. I'll stay here and meet them if they pull alongside."

"No. What if they—"

"Don't worry. Chances are, they're just like us. I seriously doubt they mean us any harm. Like you said, this is the only place left above water. Makes sense that other survivors would come here. No reason we can't share it. But just in case, I want you to be out of harm's way."

Penny started to protest, but she read Leigh's expression. This was important to him. He'd been unable to protect her and the baby from the rising floodwaters. The weather was out of his control. These new arrivals weren't. Despite her better judgment, she conceded.

The boat's motor grew louder. Penny quickly ducked behind a damp stack of cardboard boxes. She peeked out at Leigh. He winked at her, and then turned his attention back to the people in the boat. She could tell by his stance that he was nervous. That made two of them. Three, counting the baby.

"It will be okay," she whispered.

The motor abruptly died. Silence ensued.

"Hello, inside!" A man's voice—a deep, pleasant baritone.

Penny shivered, but didn't know why.

"Hello," Leigh yelled, raising his hand. "Are you okay?"

"Certainly," the man called back. "May we come inside? It would be nice to get out of the rain. We have food we can share."

Penny's misgivings vanished at the thought of something other than Tim Tams to eat.

"Leave your weapons onboard," Leigh said. "If you don't

mind, that is?"

"We'd rather not leave them out here in the water, if it's all the same to you. If it will make you feel better, how about we unload them first?"

Leigh nodded tentatively. "Well, I guess that would be okay. Hang on. I'll throw down the rope ladder."

One by one, the three castaways ascended into the chapel tower. Penny watched from her hiding place. They stood by the window, water streaming from their ponchos. When they threw back their hoods, she got a better look. There were three men. One was Caucasian, and in his thirties. The second was dark complexioned, possibly of Arabic or Hispanic descent, and in his forties. The third man was Black, and seemingly ageless. A tuft of curly black hair hung from his chin. Two of the men carried rifles and the third had a pistol. They smiled at Leigh.

The black man stepped forward and offered his free hand. "Mr. Haig, I presume?"

His voice identified him as the speaker she'd heard before. Penny watched, biting her lip.

Leigh glanced at the man's outstretched hand, and then at the rifle. "H-how do you know my name?"

"Divination. But that's not important. Is Penny with you? We'd love to meet her as well."

Leigh tried to speak. Instead, he uttered a frightened and confused squawk. Penny put her hands protectively over her belly.

"Look," Leigh stammered. "What's going on here? How do you know about us? Who are you? Are you with the authorities?"

The black man nodded. "In a manner of speaking. But not your government, I'm afraid."

"Americans?"

"At one time. But now, not really. More like the United Nations, but in all actuality, we don't answer to them, either. We're with Black Lodge. Are you familiar with the name?"

Leigh shook his head.

"No matter," the man continued. "We've traveled for

several days to find you. You may call me Mr. Raston. These are my associates, Mr. Stein and Mr. Ahmad. We really need to speak with you and Penny. Is she available?"

"No," Leigh said, backing slowly away. "She's not here. She...drowned."

The white guy, Stein, smiled. His teeth reminded Penny of a shark's.

"Unless I'm mistaken," he said, "she's hiding behind those boxes over there in the corner."

Leigh's hands curled into fists. "You just stay the fuck away from her."

Taking a deep breath, Penny stood up and stepped out of hiding. "I'm here."

"Ah," Raston said, "it's very nice to meet you, Miss Khaw."

"What do you want?"

"Well, that's the rub of it."

"What do you want?" she asked again.

He leaned the rifle against the wall and spread his arms out wide. "Just your baby. That's all. We just need your baby."

Penny gaped at them. Her eyes were wide, her fists clenched.

Leigh took a deep breath. "What?"

"Penny is thirteen weeks pregnant," Raston said. "There is a shortage of babies right now. Indeed, there's a shortage of everyone. It's nothing personal. She just happens to be one of the last pregnant woman on Earth, and we need your baby."

Leigh positioned himself between the men and Penny. He felt naked and vulnerable against the armed intruders, but tried not to let it show.

"Get the hell out of here. Right now."

Raston's tone changed. "Mr. Haig, I'm sorry, but it can't be avoided. There is another woman, Nahed Shahabi, who also happens to be pregnant, but we have no operatives in her area. Again, it's nothing personal. Just luck of the draw."

Leigh eyed the man's rifle, still leaning against the wall. Ahmad pointed the other rifle at them.

"Are you trying to scare us?" Leigh asked. "You can't

shoot. Remember, I watched you unload your guns before you got out of the boat."

"Perhaps," Ahmad said. His accent was thick. "Or maybe you saw what we wanted you to see. Some clever slight of hand. Do you want to take a chance?"

"You're lying."

"He's not," Raston said. His voice sounded sad.

Stein's hand crept toward the pistol in his waistband.

"Don't," Leigh warned.

Stein's expression was blank. His hand closed around the pistol's butt.

"I mean it," Leigh shouted. "Don't you fucking move!"

"Mr. Haig," Raston said softly, "you are unarmed. We have the upper hand, and Mr. Ahmad could end your life right now. But we don't want to do that. Indeed, we're just as upset about this whole thing as you are. Be reasonable. Cooperate and this will all be over soon. The fact is, your baby will save the world."

"Leave us alone," Penny sobbed.

"Stay behind me," Leigh whispered to her. Then he turned his attention back to the men. "You people are crazy. You do know that, right?"

Raston shook his head. "I wish that were true. But it's not. Our organization deals with things like this all the time. Think of us as military magicians. We deal with the things the rest of humanity is unequipped to battle. Things like what's happening outside."

"Global warming?"

"No, Mr. Haig. Apocalyptic magic run amok. Time is short, so I'll give you an abbreviated version. There are thirteen entities, neither demon nor angel, who strive for nothing but the destruction of all existence. Consider them the ultimate nihilists. They have servants on every Earth, and our world is no different. A cult in Baltimore has managed to unleash not one, but two of these thirteen entities—Leviathan and Behemoth. Neither will rest until this Earth is utterly destroyed. As we speak, their minions overrun the planet. The seas are full of Leviathan's children. On what little land is left,

Behemoth's worms leave a disease in their wake; it's a fungal infection that turns the human body into water."

"That's ridiculous."

"Is it? 'The waters wear the stones and wash away the things which grow out of the dust of the earth, and destroy the hopes of man.' That's from the book of Job, Mr. Haig. Although humanity misunderstands much of the Bible's content, that particular passage is quite telling. Everything—all solid matter—will eventually turn into water. This is how our world ends, unless my associates and I act to stop it. We need your help, as traumatic as it might be."

"Oh," Leigh whispered. "You guys need help, for sure."

He reached behind him and squeezed Penny's hand. She squeezed back, hard enough to make him wince.

"We do indeed," Raston said. "Summoning Leviathan and Behemoth—opening a doorway for them to enter our world, required an infant. A sacrifice. Banishing them and closing that doorway requires the same thing. Believe me, I wish there was another way. I really do. Black Lodge defends humanity. We don't want to do this. But unfortunately, we are bound by the spell's requirements. We need your baby, and we need it now."

Raston reached behind his back and pulled out a long combat knife. The blade looked very sharp. Penny screamed. Outside, the rain grew louder.

Leigh's eyes flashed from the knife to Ahmad's rifle. At the same time, Stein inched closer, reaching for his pistol.

"This has happened before," Raston said. He spoke quietly, as if talking to himself. "Three of our predecessors followed a star, in search of a newborn babe—the King of the Jews. Herod thought these magi did his bidding, but instead, they attempted to save the world."

Leigh squeezed Penny's hand. "Run!"

Hearing her footsteps echoing behind him, Leigh leapt forward, seizing Stein's wrist just as the man's fingers closed around the pistol butt. Leigh's momentum knocked them both to the floor. Leigh landed on top of Stein. His knee smashed into Stein's crotch. The man's breath rushed from his lungs and he moaned, going limp. His breath reeked. Leigh seized the handgun. Something zipped by Leigh's ear. A second later, he heard the explosion, realizing that Ahmad was shooting.

"No," Raston shouted. "You might hit the woman's belly! The baby is no good if it's dead."

Ears ringing, Leigh stumbled to his feet. He didn't have much experience with firearms, and wasn't very religious, but he prayed the pistol worked. As Raston ran after Penny, Leigh pointed the handgun at Ahmad and pulled the trigger. The gun jerked in his hands. Startled, Leigh almost dropped the weapon. A brass jacket flew from the side of the pistol and spun through the air. Leigh fired again. The rifle slipped from Ahmad's hands as the man toppled backward. The wall was splattered with blood. Panting, Leigh bent over and tried not to throw up. The room spun.

Groaning, Stein stumbled to his feet, cradling his groin with his hands. Leigh whirled around and pointed the pistol at him.

Stein held out his hands. "Don't—"

Leigh shot him in the chest. His aim was improving. Despite the gunshots ringing in his ears, he heard Penny scream.

"Raston," he yelled. "Leave her alone, you son of a bitch!"

He charged after them. Penny was backed into a corner, pressed up against the damp concrete wall. Raston was inches away, knife pointed at her belly.

"Hush now," he said. "I promise this will be over quickly. And I'm sorry."

Enraged, Leigh dispensed with caution and flung himself at the attacker. They tumbled to the floor. The knife skittered across the cement, coming to rest in a puddle of water beneath a leak in the chapel's roof. Leigh loomed over Raston, pressing the hot barrel of the pistol against the man's chin. Raston's eyes grew wide. Leigh tried to speak, but all that came out was a strangled growl.

Raston sighed. "You don't understand, Mr. Haig. If you kill me, you'll destroy the world."

"No," Leigh told him. "Penny and the baby are my world.

Nothing else matters."

He pulled the trigger, obliterating most of Raston's face. Gore showered down like the rain outside.

Penny ran to him. They embraced.

"He said the world would end," Penny sobbed. "What if he—"

Leigh silenced her with a kiss.

"As long as we have each other, it doesn't matter. The two of you are all the world I need."

TAKE ME TO THE RIVER

Cleveland, Ohio

I'm so fucking thirsty. Just can't seem to get enough water, which is funny, considering what's happened. Kelly said it was magic; that was the only explanation for the weather. Black magic. Maybe he was right. I mean, talk about a shitty forecast! Today, chance of rain one hundred percent with showers overnight and into tomorrow; more of the same for the rest of the week, the month—for your entire fucking life.

I saw bits and pieces on the news, but not much. The power went out pretty quick in these parts. But what I did see was horrifying. Cities flooded and people drowning, and then the cities were gone, buried beneath the waves, all within a matter of a week. Hell, entire countries got swallowed up. I'm living in the middle of Ohio and it's beachfront property now.

Yeah, a storm that powerful, and the fact that it hasn't stopped yet—that's got to be magic, I guess. Kelly knew what time it was. Of course, Kelly also dropped acid every goddamn day, so maybe he didn't know.

I don't know, you know?

It itches, this white stuff that's growing on me. Itches so bad it burns. But when I try to scratch it, something happens. The stuff does something weird. Not sure how to describe it. Calming, maybe? The fungus whispers in my brain, speaking to me.

Soft...soft...

That's what it whispers. The words are wet. Cool. Soothing. They sound like my voice, but I know it's not me that's thinking it. It's the fungus. It looks like bleached peach fuzz.

I noticed it growing on me two days ago, right after Kelly

died. God, I don't want to think about that. Something that looked like a cross between a human and a Great White shark came and bit him in half. One minute, we were shooting birds, and the next, something jumped out of the water and Kelly's lower half was standing next to me, gray and purple guts spilling out over his legs. His upper half was gone, and the thing that did it splashed back into the water. I caught a glimpse of its eyes before it vanished beneath the waves. They weren't black, like a shark's. They looked human. Intelligent.

I was splattered with Kelly's blood. Screaming, I watched his lower half totter forward. The choppy surf tossed his legs and guts around. A seagull darted down from the sky and flew away with a strand of Kelly hanging from its beak. I'm not sure what. His intestine, maybe? It looked like a purple and red worm.

I ran back inside, ripped off my clothes, and washed up. And that's when I noticed it. The fungus. There was a small patch sprouting between my toes. The white fuzz. That's what we'd heard other survivors call it. It's like a case of athlete's foot from Hell.

I'd seen it before I got it myself. The shit began sprouting up all over town about two weeks after the rains started. After everything went to hell. It was growing on things—buildings that were still above water, and people. Before the river covered Main Street, I saw a Mitsubishi flower delivery van with this shit growing all over the side of it. Saw a bird—it had thin white strands growing between his feathers. The bird didn't fly, didn't move, didn't even fall over after I shot it. It just sat on a phone wire, getting drenched. And there was a guy, too, on the roof of the movie theatre. The shit had grown over his flesh and his clothes. Covered him almost completely. His eyes were still visible, but that was all. They were like two round dots of black ink, staring out of a white, hairy human-shaped mound. He just stood there in the rain, his arms stretched upward to the sky, like some sort of weird tree, soaking up the water. The white fuzz absorbed the raindrops as they fell on him, and I swear, I heard it growing. It sounded like a bowl of Rice Krispies in milk.

The man kept saying, "*Soft.*" His voice was barely a whisper. Every time he opened his mouth, I saw that the stuff was inside of him, too, and when I shot him, instead of blood, more strands of white fuzz poked out.

He didn't fall over after I shot him, and that's when I realized that he'd taken root. The fuzz had sent out little tendrils, anchoring him to the roof. It's like he was turning into something else. I don't know what.

I don't fucking know much of anything anymore.

All I do know is that this itching is driving me crazy! I want to scratch at it, dig my fingernails into my skin and just scratch until I bleed.

Soft…soft…

There. That's better. Didn't even have to scratch.

Like I said, I didn't see much of what happened elsewhere, but here, it was fucked up. It started raining one day, around six o'clock in the morning—and just didn't stop. The power went out, and soon after, the looting began (that's how Kelly and I got all that cool stuff). The governor mobilized the National Guard, but that didn't last too long. By then, most of those soldier dudes had seen the writing on the wall. They deserted, taking their families and heading for higher ground.

The Ohio River flooded its banks and just kept right on flowing. It took out the farmlands on the outskirts of the city and then it washed over the rest, flooding the downtown district. By that time, Kelly and I had set up shop in the Sheraton's penthouse suite, so we were safe and dry. At night, we'd get stoned and listen to the rain. In the morning, we'd do more of the same. Until we ran out of weed and acid.

Thirsty. No more bottled water left, either. I drank it all. Hell, there's nothing left. All that shit we ganked during the looting; the televisions and compact discs and food and guns, all of it is gone now, taken by those fucking bikers.

I hid inside the shower when they raided the building this morning. Pulled the shower curtain closed and held my breath. I guess with all the water outside, they didn't much feel like checking the bathtub. I stayed in there while they cleaned us out. The urge to scratch got really strong, but the voice inside my head calmed me down and kept me from blowing my hiding place.

Soft...soft...

Shut the fuck up and get out of my head!

The bikers loaded up their motorboats and sped off downstream—down Main Street. And here I am.

I hope one of those shark things eats the fucking bikers.

Soft...soft...

Shit. Can't write. Can't even think. It's this fucking stuff. Will finish later. So thirsty...

Later. I must have slept all day. Feels like I hibernated or something. It's nighttime now. The moon is out, but I can barely see it through the cloud cover. It should be full tonight, if the calendar is right, but there's just a sickly yellow glow in the sky.

Soft...soft...

It's still raining. Didn't really expect anything different, I guess. Sometimes I think the constant sound of falling rain will drive me insane. It never fucking stops, man! The drops just beat against the window constantly.

I'm still thirsty. My mouth feels like cotton, and my arms and legs are numb. My head hurts. Like I'm hung over.

Soft...soft...

Shut up.

Sof—

I said shut the hell up!

There's a big white patch of fuzz on my stomach. I touched it. It's soft and cool, like moss. Soon as I probed it, the itching started again, and then it burned. I thought about getting a knife, and trying to cut it off me, but if I do that, I'm gonna lose some serious skin. Don't know if I'm strong enough to go through that. I already feel like shit. If I operate, there's a chance that I could pass out and die from blood loss.

I could shoot myself. I mean, who am I kidding? I've seen what this shit does. It grows right overtop of you, turns you into some kind of white, fuzzy plant-zombie. Yeah, maybe sucking on the end of that pistol—

Soft...soft...

—is the easy way out. But every time I reach for the pistol, the fungus starts burning again. So I'm pretty much fucked.

Soft...soft...

But now it doesn't seem to itch anymore, so that's okay.

Soft...soft...

Wish I could figure out what it wants. It's driving me crazy. Chattering in my head every few seconds. Just repeating that word over and over again. I'm so fucking thirsty!

Soft...soft...

Is that it? It needs water?

SOFT...SOFT...

That's it, isn't it? You need water? Well fuck you, fungus. You can't have any. There's a whole river right outside the door, but you're not—

What's it doing now? It...I can feel...*soft*...feel it inside my...*soft*...head, doing something...*soft*...going to...*soft*... go outside...*soft*...for a while...*soft*...and look at...*soft*... the moon...*soft*...and...*soft*...stand...*soft*...by the...*soft*...by the...*soft*...banks of the river.

No! What am I saying? Look at this—it's even showing up in my writing. I didn't write that. This white fuzz did. There is no riverbank. The water is all the way—

SOFT...SOFT...SOFT...SOFT...

Oh...

Oh, that's nice. That feels better. Much better. Going to go outside now and stand next to the river. I like the water. The water is nice. The water is...

It's soft.

Soft.

Soft...

THE END
OF SOLITUDE

Somewhere in the New Atlantic

Jade Rumsey couldn't swim. She'd taken lessons last year and they didn't help. She still sank like a rock. That was strike one. Strikes two and three were that she was terrified of water and knew nothing about boats. And here she was, floating above Michigan on a massive, abandoned tugboat that had drifted down from the Great Lakes.

At least she had books. And food. And books. And clean water. And books.

She'd been perched on her roof, soaked to the bone and shivering, watching the water rise higher, when the tugboat crashed into her house. The roof collapsed. Screaming, Jade slid towards the water, breaking her fingernails on the tiles. She'd tumbled onto the tugboat's rain-slicked deck, knocking the air from her lungs. Jade passed out, raindrops beating against her face.

When she woke, the tugboat was still riding the waves. Her roof was nowhere in sight. The few rooftops and cell phone towers jutting from the water didn't look familiar. Shaking, Jade stood up. The deck pitched and heaved beneath her feet. She stumbled to the cabin, shouting for help, but her cries went unanswered. The cabin was deserted, as was the rest of the boat.

She was adrift and alone.

Her spirits soared after searching the tugboat. The cabin was dry, if not warm. There was ample food and bottled water. Blankets and medical supplies. More importantly, there were lots of books. Jade loved to read, so much, in fact, that she'd even started her own small press publishing company—Solitude Publications—just to work with some of the authors she admired. Apparently, the tugboat's crew had shared her passion, if not her exact tastes. There were three boxes of paperbacks onboard, as well as a box of hardcovers and another containing porn magazines. She was a little disappointed that there was no Richard Laymon, Michael Marshall Smith, or Charles De Lint, but she did find some Stephen King and Dean Koontz novels, along with various westerns, crime novels, James Patterson and Tom Clancy titles, and a bunch of Readers Digest condensed books. She sighed, wishing for something better. Still, anything to read was better than nothing to read. The porn was an especially good find. Strictly old school—not like looking at it online.

Jade settled in. It was the end of the world, but she felt fine, all things considered. She avoided going outside, and stayed in the cabin, reading and sleeping and enjoying herself as best she could. With no engine or navigation, the tugboat wandered aimlessly, propelled by the current. Occasionally it bumped into wreckage, but for most of the time, it floated freely.

Jade saw no survivors. She missed her cat and her house and her 1995 Cougar, but tried not to think about them. At night, the rain drummed against the decks and bulkheads, lulling her to sleep.

The boat had a working radio; it was a massive, confusing thing, much bigger than a standard AM/FM receiver. Jade experimented with it until she learned how to operate it. When the silence became oppressive, she'd scan the dial, searching for signs that she wasn't the last person left alive. Usually, there was silence, but twice she'd picked up a static-filled broadcast from Boston. The speaker, Mark, was apparently sick with some kind of fungal infection. He sent a warning to anyone receiving his signal. The disease supposedly turned people into fungal zombies, and eventually, broke them down into nothing more than water. Whether it was true or not, Mark obviously believed it was happening to him. His voice made her sad. He kept asking for his wife and son. Both times, she'd turned him off and went back to reading.

Jade enjoyed her solitude.

Until the men came.

They boarded the tugboat on the fifth night, when the full moon was just a pale, silver disc, barely visible through the cloud cover. Jade heard their motor and woke up in time to see them pulling alongside—shadows in the darkness. They tossed two grappling hooks over the bow and climbed aboard. There were six of them, and she saw more figures still milling about on the other boat. With the rain and gloom, she couldn't make out their features. The only thing she could see clearly were the rifles they carried. Jade didn't know much about guns, but these looked big. Scary. Rain dripped from the barrels.

She ducked down beneath the window and held her breath. Footsteps splashed across the deck. There was a flare gun in the storage locker to her left, but she didn't know how to use it. A fire extinguisher hung on the wall to her right. Slowly, she reached for it.

The cabin door burst open. Gusts of rain and wind blew into the room. A large man stood silhouetted in the doorway, pointing a gun at her head. He was at least six feet tall, and big, like a linebacker. His ruddy face was covered with the stubbly growth of a new beard. Water dripped from his chin. His eyes were red and rheumy. When he spoke, his voice was like granite.

"Howdy."

Jade blinked. "H-hello."

She wondered if he was friendly or dangerous.

Without taking his eyes from her, the man spoke to the others behind him. "Jackpot, boys. Got us some top-shelf pussy here. Still alive, too."

This was greeted with raucous cheers.

Dangerous, Jade decided. Her stomach fluttered. Her heart rate increased. The fire extinguisher was just inches away, but she was afraid to reach for it.

"I don't want any trouble," she said, trying to sound unafraid.

"Don't really care what you want." The man strode into the cabin, still leveling the rifle at her. "In case you ain't noticed, it's a new world out there. Far as we're concerned, you don't get a say."

Jade shrank away from him, pressing herself against the bulkhead. More men filed into the cabin, leaving wet footprints. Water dripped from their hats and coats. Each of them was armed. They stared at her, leering. One of the men shined a flashlight into her eyes. Jade cringed.

The big man glanced around the cabin. "The hell is this shit? Nothing but books? Where's everything else?"

Jade struggled to find her voice. "What are you looking for?"

"Food. Water. Others." He grinned. "Any more like you onboard?"

She shook her head. "No."

The man with the flashlight crept closer. He was shorter than the leader and smelled like an open sewer. He grasped her chin with his dirty, sausage-like fingers.

"I call first dibs," he said.

The big man's speed belied his size. He brought the rifle up and smashed the stock against the smaller man's chin, knocking him to the floor. Shattered teeth rolled across the tiles. The other men gasped and giggled.

"Motherfucker," the big man snarled. "You'd best remember who the alpha dog is."

A sudden jolt jarred them all. The tugboat shuddered. Storage lockers flew open, their contents spilling all over the floor. Several of the startled men lost their footing. Others crashed against the bulkhead, crying out. Jade bit her lip, refusing to show fear.

"The fuck," the big man shouted. "What was that?"

"We hit something," one of the other men said.

Out on the deck, somebody screamed.

"Get out there," the big man ordered. "See what the hell is happening."

They charged back out into the rain. The big man knelt and checked the fallen man's pulse.

"Still alive," he muttered. "Serves you right, though. Trying to claim her for yourself."

More screams from outside, followed by a whipping sound.

Standing, the big man turned to Jade. "Thought you were alone?"

"I am."

"We'll see. Stay here or I'll gut you."

Jade clasped her arms around her shoulders and shivered, watching as the man walked out onto the lurching deck. As he did, a long, serpentine shadow lashed out of the darkness, coiled around his head, and squeezed. The big man had time to utter one muffled shriek and then the top of his head exploded. His brains showered down onto his shoulders. Jade screamed.

More tentacles appeared, probing the cabin's interior. Jade fell silent as they slithered across the floor. Her lip trembled as one drew close. Then they retreated. Outside, the battle continued. Gunshots and screams peppered the night.

Jade stood on trembling legs and stumbled to the door. She stepped out into the rain. At the front of the tugboat, the men fought more tentacles. She couldn't see what they were connected to—the appendages simply appeared out of the fog and rain.

The tugboat tilted sharply to one side. Jade gripped the rail and watched the ocean's surface creep closer. The water churned and bubbled. A tendril slapped down on the rail next to her, tearing the metal bar free and hauling it beneath the surface. The deck tilted more. Something groaned. Jade smelled diesel fuel.

The boat was sinking. And with it, her last refuge. Sighing, Jade closed her eyes. She wished those swimming lessons had worked better. Then she chose the least of her fears and jumped over the side.

Within minutes, she'd found solitude again.

BEST LAID PLANS

Landrum, South Carolina

"Trust me," Scott Eubanks had told his wife, Donna. "I've got a plan."

And he had—until now.

They'd been okay, at first. Their home was in the foothills, and although the water rose steadily, it hadn't reached them. Scott and Donna hunkered down with their two dachshunds, Ketchup and Marlin, and rode the storm out. The wind and rain pummeled the house, and a particularly vicious tornado uprooted most of the trees, but they'd escaped unscathed. The power was out, but they had plenty of canned food, dry goods, and water. To stay warm, they had blankets and body heat. The dogs slept with them; this wasn't unusual. Ketchup and Marlin were Scott and Donna's de facto children. For entertainment, they had Scott's massive book collection and his guitars (he'd once played in a roots rock and pop band called Best Laid Plans). At night, the four of them cuddled up in bed together and Scott strummed—unplugged.

It wasn't so bad, for the end of the world.

They also had a battery-operated radio. Occasionally, they picked up a faint signal all the way from Boston—some guy named Mark Sylva who warned his audience about a strange white fungus that turned people into mindless drones before their bodies literally melted. The broadcaster was apparently infected with this disease. Sometimes he'd make sense—talk about a baseball and bat he'd owned, both of which were signed by the entire 2004 Red Sox team. But most of the time, his broadcasts were less lucid.

"Water," he'd gasp, his voice strained and phlegmy. "I need water...soft..."

He said that Boston was underwater—that the ocean had swallowed it up. He also babbled about things in the water—mermaids and man-sharks and carnivorous flying fish and giant, squid-headed demigods. Donna usually made Scott turn the radio off when this happened.

"I don't like it," she'd say. "That poor man. What if we end up like that?"

"We'll be fine," Scott said. "You'll see. I've got a plan."

But he didn't. Not really.

The rain kept falling and the water kept rising. Nobody showed up to rescue them. Realizing that the house would soon flood, Scott made plans—plans for their evacuation.

He'd grown up in Mobile, Alabama, but when he was thirteen, his mother had remarried and they moved to York, Pennsylvania. His mother still lived there. He often wondered if she was okay, but had no way of knowing. His father's family was from Landrum, and Scott had moved back seven years ago. Since then, he'd learned the area well. He planned their evacuation with the local geography in mind. Landrum was on the outskirts of two major cities, high-priced Greenville and working class Spartanburg. Scott worked in Spartanburg as a programmer for a company that wrote software for pharmacies.

They needed to reach high ground, and had several options. Their home was in the foothills of the Saluda Grade, leading up into the Blue Ridge Mountains. Glassy Mountain was ten miles away. If they could make it to Spartanburg, the Beacon might provide shelter. It was an old drive-in grease joint that had been around for decades, and was located on high ground. If they traveled west on I-26, they could reach Asheville, North Carolina, which was up in the mountains. Asheville was considered the San Francisco of the south due to its thriving gay community. It was a very artsy town and had a great music hall—the Orange Peel—where Scott had once seen Henry Rollins perform. If they had to pick where they would survive the apocalypse, Asheville was Scott's top choice.

After he'd planned their location, he considered travel.

Some type of transport was required. No way could he and Donna go on foot, especially not with Ketchup and Marlin. Leaving the dogs behind wasn't even a consideration. Both animals were almost ten years old, and not as spry as they'd once been. If the roads were flooded—and there was a good chance they would be—they'd have to steal a boat. Scott had driven pontoons and motorboats in the past, and he knew how to swim.

The plans crystallized in his head.

Plan A: While Donna packed food, water, and gear, he'd go outside, and see what the roads were like. If they were flooded, he'd find a boat (somebody in the neighborhood had to have a bass boat, at the very least). Once he'd stolen it, they'd escape to Asheville.

Plan B: If he couldn't find a boat, they'd head up into the hills and hide out in the upper extremes of the Blue Ridge Mountains. Maybe they could find a hunting cabin or something. The only problem with this plan was that they'd have to carry the dogs.

Donna busied herself with packing, and Scott went on a scouting expedition. He selected a golf club and kitchen knife for defense. He walked out into the storm, and despite his protective raingear, he was immediately drenched. Shivering, he plodded on, surveying the damage to the neighborhood. Most of the vegetation was gone. Once lush yards were now mud-filled swamps. Trees and shrubs lay on their sides, their roots unable to find purchase in the sodden ground. The flooding was worse than he'd imagined. Everywhere he went, the rushing waters were at least ankle-deep. Several times, he sank up to his knees and the force of the current almost swept him away.

Scott was just about to turn back and go with Plan B, when he saw the man. He stood about twenty feet away, partially obscured by the steady downpour and swirling mist.

"Hey," Scott yelled. "Good to see you. I thought we were the only ones left."

The figure made no reply.

Scott sloshed towards him. "You okay? My name's Scott.

My wife and I were planning on heading up into the hills. You wouldn't happen to have access to a boat, would you?"

The man still didn't respond. As Scott drew closer, he saw why. The strangers face was completely grown over with white, fuzzy mold. It obscured his mouth and nose. His eyes were two sunken pinpricks of grey. The fungus also covered his arms. Scott glanced down at the man's feet and saw white, root-like appendages dipping into the flowing water.

"Jesus Christ!"

The fuzz split open, revealing a pale, toothless mouth. The creature's voice was like a whisper without the sound.

"*Soft...*"

Scott didn't know what that meant, and didn't care. He turned to flee, then skidded to a halt. More of the things emerged from hiding—men, women, children, and even a dog. All of them were covered with the same disgusting growth. They quickly surrounded him. Scott's pulse throbbed in his ears. The guy on the radio had been right.

The closest figure reached for him. Scott lashed out with the golf club, swinging with all his strength. The makeshift weapon struck the fungal creature in the head, which promptly exploded, turning to water. The stench was nauseating—not rancid, but cloying and damp. Musky. Retching, Scott backed away from it. He brought up the golf club for another strike, but it was too late. The creatures reached for him with their wet, slimy, mold-covered appendages. His skin burned and itched where they touched him. Scott screamed.

They fell on him. Scott collapsed beneath their weight, sinking into the churning waters, struggling to keep his head above the surface. Their grasp felt like wet leaves. He gasped for air. They forced him back down, pawing at him. Several of the monsters burst as he fought with them, soaking him even more.

Scott's head slipped beneath the water, and his last thought was that while he'd planned for the weather, he'd never planned for this.

THE SKY
IS CRYING

Somewhere in the New North Sea

King's Lynn (or just "Lynn" as the locals referred to it), had
been located on England's east coast. It was a historic port
town with a population of just over thirty-six thousand people.
Since it was situated along the seaside, it never stood a chance.

The first wave crashed over the Boal Quay docks and
swept them out to sea. Then the harbor was engulfed.
Subsequent waves eradicated everything along the shoreline—
houses, shops, people. Within days, the tide had crept three
miles inland, surrounding the Queen Elizabeth hospital and
submerging the rest of the town. King's Lynn's population
was now down to a few dozen.

And all of them were living on this ship.

Jason Houghton stared up at the sky. The sky was crying,
just like in the song. Jason was a big fan of pre-war American
Blues. No other type of music carried such an emotional
impact. He closed his eyes against the storm. The ship rolled
beneath his feet, and his stomach lurched. He'd never had
much experience with boats, and had been seasick the first
few days. He'd eaten crackers to ease the nausea. The wind
rolled in over the flight deck, tossing his wet hair and blowing
cold rain against his face. He listened to it howl and shivered.
To Jason, the wind sounded like Stevie Ray Vaughn.

He knew that he should go inside, get out of the rain. The
big thing to worry about was hypothermia. It could be avoided
for the most part if you stayed dry. But once you got wet…

Of course, they didn't have to worry about that now.

Before the Royal Navy had arrived, Lynn's survivors had
all taken shelter in the upper floors of the hospital. Jason and
his girlfriend Catherine had been among them, since they

both worked for the hospital. Jason was a hospital computer system administrator—a job that was about as exciting as it sounded. The hospital was located on the river estuary, where The Great Ouse met the North Sea. Even as the survivors huddled together near the top, the waters continued to rise. If the rescuers hadn't shown up when they did, all would have been lost. The Royal Navy had sent out an expeditionary force of small boats, searching for survivors. They found them atop the hospital, frantically waving bed sheets from the roof. The sailors had transported the survivors, including Jason and Catherine, back to a bigger vessel with a helicopter flight deck and big guns capable of shelling land fortifications in time of war.

Jason heard a motor sputter to life. It jarred him from his memories. He glanced down at the ocean's surface. They were launching small boats again, sending them out to search for more survivors. Six of them sailed away, heading in different directions. The crew couldn't take the bigger ship into flooded areas because of all the buildings and things beneath the water. These new, manmade reefs could rip the ship's side open if they tried. Above, the sky continued to weep. Jason was just about to go inside, dry off, and find Catherine, when he saw something on the horizon.

The constant rain played havoc with visibility. Between the haze, mist, and lack of sunlight, the ocean was a gloomy place, full of shadows. The horizon was often dark, even during daylight. But now, something darker than the darkness around it was moving around out there on the ocean's surface.

A black wave.

"What…?"

It rolled closer, moving against the current. It was the same size as the other waves on the sea. Amazingly, raindrops slid down its surface rather than being absorbed. One of the small boats changed course and roared towards the oddity, intent on investigating. The wave changed its course to match them, and increased its speed. Before the crew could maneuver out of the way, the wave crashed over their boat, swamping it. When it moved on, the boat was gone and the wave had doubled in size.

"Men overboard," Jason shouted. "Men overboard!"

On the ship, other crew members and civilians ran to the rails, attracted by his shouts. Down on the sea, the other small boats zipped towards the area of the missing craft. The black wave rushed to meet them. It surged over another boat. Several crewmembers tried to leap aside, but the black water sucked them into the wave's mass. They vanished, just like the previous crew. So did the second boat. And again, the wave seemed to swell. It changed course once more, flowing smoothly against the tide, cutting through the regular waves.

An alarm bell rang out, followed by a series of sharp, high-pitched whistles. The ship now bustled with activity. Jason felt someone grab his arm. He spun around and stared into Catherine's face.

"What's happening?" she asked.

"It's…" He motioned at the water, unable to continue.

The wave took out a third craft. This time, it was close enough to clearly see the details of the attack. It quivered as it flowed over the boat. Both the sailors and the boat seemed to liquefy. The wave absorbed them both; it drew them into its mass, converting them into more dark water.

The remaining search and rescue boats veered back towards the ship. Their crewmembers were panicked and screaming. The wave changed course again, turning in a wide arc, and chased after them. It was much bigger now than it had been when Jason first spotted it. Along the rails, the onlookers gasped and shrieked.

Jason grabbed Catherine's hand. "Come on!"

"Where are we going?"

"I don't know," he said. "Back to our cabin!"

She halted, pulling him. "That won't help. You saw what it did to the little boat."

"Well, then what do you suggest? We swim?"

Catherine was a strong swimmer. Jason could make do, but not for long.

She shook her head. "I don't know. We just—"

The rest of Catherine's reply was cut off by her sobs.

Tears ran down her rain-slicked face. Jason pulled her close and held her. Around them, the screams increased. Jason lifted Catherine's face to his. He gently closed her eyes with his fingertip. Then he closed his own. Sighing, he kissed her.

"I love you," he whispered.

"I love you, too."

The wave rushed towards them, and crashed over the rails, engulfing the ship.

The sky continued to weep.

DAWN OF
THE DORSALS

Somewhere in the New Pacific

William King's stomach heaved again. He wanted to puke, but he hadn't eaten in days. All that came out was a thin strand of saliva. His raw throat burned. The boat rolled beneath him, tossed by another wave. William clung to the pitching deck. He was seasick. Although, given the condition of the world around him, perhaps worldsick was a better term, because that's what the world was now—one big, giant sea.

The pale, silver disc of the sun climbed into the sky, casting its muted light through the downpour, signaling the start of another dreary day. Thunder rumbled in the distance like a rooster greeting the dawn.

William groaned. More cramps shot through him. His stomach clenched and unclenched like a fist. He was so dizzy, he couldn't even stand. It felt like the boat was spinning around like a carousel.

"Oh, God," he moaned. "Make it stop."

From their dry spot in the cabin, his three cats—Hunter, Boo, and Ally—watched him with expressions varying from casual indifference to wide-eyed dismay through the foggy window.

Eventually, the nausea passed. William stumbled to his feet, careful not to slip on the rain-slicked deck. He began slowly making his way back to the cabin, thinking of his mother, Carol, and his sister, Pari, as he walked. They'd been in Lake Oswego, Oregon, when the rains began. William had been vacationing at his home away from home—a three-bedroom rancher sat on the outskirts of Snyder, Oklahoma. Now he was somewhere between the two, adrift on this vast, seemingly endless ocean in a stolen boat, with just the cats for company. He'd seen no other survivors. Indeed, he'd seen very few living creatures. A few sickly birds soared through the sky. Occasionally, fish would break the ocean's surface. A few nights ago, he'd thought he saw a woman, far off in the distance, and heard a snatch of song—but then the rain's pace had increased and the vision vanished.

Still thinking about that, William opened the cabin door and went inside. He slipped out of his wet clothes and put on his only other set, which were still a little damp from the day before. Hunter and Boo greeted him with meows and purrs. Ally glanced at him and then looked away. He reached down and scratched Hunter behind the ears. The gray tabby arched its back and purred louder. Ally watched this, then turned her nose up with disdain. The cabin smelled of cat piss and feces. William pissed in a bucket and tossed it overboard when it was full. The cats had no such luxury.

William's earlier thoughts returned. It was entirely possible that he and the cats might be the last things left alive—other than the birds and fish.

"If that's true," he told the small calico, "then you need to start being nicer."

Ally responded with a hiss. William realized that she wasn't looking at him, but beyond him. He turned and stared out the window. It was covered with condensation, and visibility was limited. He wiped it with his hand and peered harder. Then he gasped.

They weren't the last things left alive, after all. Several sleek, triangular dorsal fins parted the water and glided towards them. He knew what they were immediately. Sharks. And big ones, judging by the size of the fins. William looked out the other windows and saw more of them approaching. The boat was surrounded. The dorsal fins quickly bore down on it. The largest fin was possibly six feet high. William paled, wondering how big the rest of the creature must be.

Ally hissed again, showing her displeasure. For once, William agreed with her. He grabbed the fire axe and the pistol (both had been left behind by the boat's previous owner) and headed back out into the rain. The sea spray soaked through his clothing. He made his way to the rail and peered over the edge. The fins were circling the boat now, and William glimpsed the figures beneath them—long, gray shadows, swimming like bullets.

"Get out of here," he shouted, banging on the rail with the axe. "Go on! Scat."

Too late, he remembered that sharks had extra sensitive hearing and could detect sounds from miles away. He couldn't remember where he knew that from—some television documentary he'd glimpsed in passing, probably.

Okay, he thought. *What else do I know about sharks?* The theme from the movie Jaws ran through his head. *Think, goddamn it!* They were supposed to have really superb olfactory senses, weren't they? They could smell blood from miles away. And if you hit them in the snout, it was supposed to hurt them. Like kicking a man in the balls. The snout—and the eyes. Those were the weak spots. Or stop it from swimming. He was pretty sure that if a shark stopped swimming, it died.

"Can you all stop swimming, please?"

The boat suddenly shuddered as something jarred the hull from beneath. William toppled over, sliding across the deck. The axe slipped from his hands, but he managed to keep his grip on the pistol. Inside the cabin, the cats howled. He heard glass break, but had no time to wonder what it was because something slammed into the hull again, wrenching the entire craft to the starboard side. The dorsal fins reappeared, circling faster and closer. Blinking the rain from his eyes, William fired at one of them, aiming for the fin. The pistol jerked in his hands, and the target vanished beneath the waves. He couldn't tell if he hit it or not.

He was just about to shoot again when the water exploded. A figure launched itself from the ocean, flew through the air, and landed on the deck. William screamed. It had the head, upper body, dorsal fin, and tail of a Great White shark, and the arms and legs of a human being. The creature stood over ten-feet tall, and must have weighed several hundred pounds. The boat listed to one side from the extra weight. It regarded him with black, soulless eyes. Then it opened its mouth, revealing rows of razor sharp teeth. The bullet-shaped head stretched toward him on a human neck. William aimed for the snout. The man-shark's roar drowned out the gun blast. It bled like a human being.

The boat shuddered and groaned. William turned around and saw that more of the creatures had jumped aboard. He fired again and again, panicked, not bothering to aim. He kept squeezing the trigger even after the gun clicked empty. Then the feeding frenzy began and the boat's deck turned red.

The ocean's surface was alive with activity as more dorsal fins appeared to greet the dawn.

DATE NIGHT

Somewhere in the New Atlantic

When the end of the world came to Land O' Lakes, Florida, it came quickly. Located less than ten miles from the ocean, Land O' Lakes' name was certainly apt. There were more ponds, lakes, bogs, swamps and pools in the town than there were retirement communities and restaurants. Or, at least there had been at one time. Now, all those various bodies of water had joined together, engulfing most of the state and submerging it under hundreds of feet of churning waves. The Atlantic Ocean was a lot bigger these days.

And Tony and Kim were in the center of it.

There hadn't been time for them to evacuate. The super storms blew in from the east, west and south without much advance warning, razing buildings with two hundred mile per hour winds and dumping over ten feet of rain in twenty-four hours. Millions in Florida and the other gulf states were killed. Those that didn't die during the storms passed away in the devastating aftermath.

Tony and Kim had been lucky. At first, they'd assumed the rains were just that—a passing summer storm. When the rain started, they were inside Camelot Books—the bookstore they owned and operated—stocking a new Edward Lee exclusive. But then came the hurricane warnings, and the "Breaking News" logos dominated the cable news screens and the fire sirens whined mournfully—then fell silent. Somehow, the sudden stillness was worse. The storm's full fury struck. Screams echoed outside, almost lost beneath the howling winds. Crashes reverberated throughout the night.

Even as the chaos mounted, they'd stayed calm. Before Tony and Kim converted it, the building had been an old

GTE switching station. The walls were sixteen inches thick and built to withstand hurricane force winds. A glass atrium, now blocked off with plywood and empty bookshelves, stood at the front of the store. It was as much a fortress as it was a bookstore. But despite its sturdiness, the building couldn't withstand the super storms. Neither did the town. By the time the bookstore's roof started rattling, Land O' Lakes had become one big lake.

When water began to pour into the building, Tony and Kim fled out into the flooded streets. The winds had died down by then, but the downpour persisted. They glanced around, shocked at the magnitude of the destruction. The old United Methodist church that had stood next to the bookstore was nothing more than a pile of rubble. A runaway sailboat—a sloop with one mast and two sails—adrift from whatever dock it had been tied to, floated down the street. They managed to hop onboard the unmanned craft. Doing so had saved their lives.

Since then, they'd floated on the roiling seas and tried to make the best of their situation. In the first few days, they'd scavenged weapons and food from the floodwaters and other abandoned boats. Once they were relatively secure, they'd simply passed the time, adapting to this new way of life.

Kim thought about all this as she sat near the foresail, staring out into the darkness. They'd rigged a tarp so that the rain wouldn't fall on them. She peeked around the tarp and glanced up at the night sky, longing for a glimpse of the stars or moon. Neither was likely. These days, the skies were a perpetual grey, and the sun and moon were hazy, vague shadows.

The breeze shifted and she fanned her nose. Corpses still floated on the ocean's surface, caught in the converging tides, endlessly circling above the drowned cities. It seemed amazing to her—Orlando, Tampa, Miami, Fort Myers—all gone. All at the bottom of the ocean. The scope of the devastation should have been daunting—terrifying—but Kim didn't let it worry her. What would be the point? There was nothing she could do to change it now. And besides, as long as she had Tony, she felt safe and secure.

Before they'd opened Camelot Books, Tony had owned a gun shop. He knew how to defend himself and how to provide for them both. And he'd done a remarkable job so far, making sure they had food and water, safeguarding them from scavengers and pirates and ocean predators, making sure she was comfortable and loved. He always knew what to do, no matter what the situation.

Despite its cramped quarters and the fact that it had none of their personal belongings, the sailboat now felt like home. This surprised Kim, but again, a big factor in her comfort was Tony. She missed their home, of course, but this wasn't so bad—all things considered. She wasn't afraid of the water. She and Tony were both good swimmers. And they were both competent with the sailboat. They'd had experience with everything from rowboats up to, and including, ski boats.

She felt a dark shadow pass beneath the hull. She couldn't see it, of course, but she sensed it just the same. Her skin prickled a bit, but she ignored it. With Tony onboard, she felt safe.

She heard him come up behind her, and sighed as he wrapped his arms around her waist, squeezing gently. Kim leaned back into him and closed her eyes. The stubble on Tony's face felt rough. He smelled of sea salt and sweat. Kim assumed that she did, too, though he hadn't mentioned it. Their showers were limited to standing on the deck in the rain with a bar of soap. She breathed deep, finding his musky scent intoxicating—a welcome change from the stench wafting off the ocean. When she heard glass clinking, she opened her eyes and turned around.

Tony smiled. "Surprise. Look what I found."

He held up a green, long-necked glass bottle. It glinted in the light of the battery-operated lantern.

Kim gasped. "Is that wine?"

"Sparkling cider, actually. I found it floating on the waves this morning, while you were sleeping. But beggars can't be choosers. It will have to do."

He popped the cork. It sounded very loud in the darkness.

Out on the water, something splashed.

"What's the occasion?" Kim asked.

"It's date night," Tony said. "But we'll have to drink from the bottle. I couldn't find any glasses."

Kim laughed. "Date night?"

"Yeah. See, I've been thinking. We've known each other since, well, since forever."

Kim nodded. It did seem like forever. Tony had been the best man at Kim's first wedding and she'd been the matron of honor at his first wedding. Neither marriage had lasted, and they'd turned to each other—helping each other through their respective divorces. After that, their friendship had just naturally grown, until one day when they looked at each other and decided that they were being silly and should really just be together. She mentioned this to Tony when he asked her what she was thinking.

"Yeah," he said. "That's my point. Because of that, we never really had a traditional first date, did we?"

"No," Kim agreed. "I guess we didn't."

"I thought maybe we should tonight. After all, it's sort of a new world, right? A new beginning. But we're still together. We're alive and we still have each other. We should honor it somehow."

He handed her the bottle. "To us."

"To us," she said, and sipped. The cider tasted good, but irritated the little sores around her mouth, brought on from vitamin deficiency.

"I love you, Kim."

"I love you, too."

She passed the bottle back to him, and Tony drank. He wiped his chapped lips with the back of his hand.

"I'll love you till the end of the world," he promised.

Kim giggled. "It already is the end of the world."

"Then I'll love you till the next time it ends."

They snuggled together, warm and content, and as they sailed into the night, the rain did not fall on them.

DEATH BY COOKIES

Redford, Michigan

There was fungus growing on Mark Beauchamp, and he knew what it wanted.

Water.

Before the batteries died in his radio, Mark had been listening to a pirate radio station in Boston. With no other signals cluttering the airwaves, it had reached all the way to Michigan. According to the broadcaster (also named Mark) the white fungus was sentient. It took you over slowly, starting out like a rash and growing steadily, until it controlled your movements and thoughts. It needed water to grow. Deprive it of water and you could halt its progress. The guy on the radio had found other ways of fighting it, as well. Most of them involved bodily harm. Burning it off. Cutting it off, along with the skin beneath it. Acid.

But Mark had found another way—eating.

He wished that the phones were still working. If they had been, he'd have called Boston and told the other Mark. All you had to do to defeat the white fuzz was to eat. The fungus didn't like that.

Soft... it whispered inside his head. *Soft...soft...* The words were cool and soothing. They sounded like his voice, but he knew better. The words belonged to the shit growing on him—and inside of him.

Mark was thirsty again. No matter how much he drank, it never seemed to be enough. Of course, now that he knew it thrived on water, he'd been dehydrating himself on purpose. The fungus didn't like that, either.

Soft...soft...soft...

Outside, the falling rain sounded delightful. How

wonderful would it be to go out there right now, and look up at the sky, and open his mouth, and drink? Just strip naked and let the rain cascade over him, lathering his body. Soaking in…

The vision seemed very real. He could almost feel the cold and the wetness. Gritting his teeth, Mark ignored the insistent urgings. That wasn't what he wanted. That was the fungus, trying to take control again. He tasted blood. His teeth were loose. Mark asserted dominance again by thinking of his wife, Paula, their four kids, and their new grandbaby (their oldest daughter had recently given birth to a beautiful seven pound baby girl named Shannon). All of them were safe, evacuated with the rest of the civilians on the National Guard's last trip through. Mark hadn't gone with them. The infection was already obvious at that point—tendrils of bleached peach fuzz had sprouted from his chin and between his fingers. The soldiers had orders to leave behind anybody who showed signs of fungal contamination. When he protested, they assured Mark that a team of biological experts would assist him once the area was evacuated and quarantined.

But those experts had never arrived. Mark doubted they ever would. There was no way to reach him, except by boat. The Detroit River was an ocean now, and his home was a slowly sinking island. The interior smelled dank and musty. The furniture and their other belongings were ruined. Mildew covered everything, along with more of the white fuzz; it was spreading across the walls and ceiling, their framed wedding picture, the kid's rooms, and on Paula's houseplants, as well. Soon it would cover everything. He wondered what would happen then.

The white fuzz itched so bad that it burned, but each time Mark tried to scratch it, something happened. The fungus released something into his system. A sedative, perhaps? Whatever it was, it calmed him, soothing his nerves so that he wouldn't scratch the substance from his flesh. It had other methods of dealing with revolt, too. Pain—a bolt of which lashed through him now. Water would stop the pain. All he had to do was get some water.

Shaking his head, he glanced down at his legs. Mark was

perched atop the kitchen counter, trying to stay above the rising water level. The fuzz had sent pale, tendril-like roots from his legs to the floor, soaking up the water seeping in from outside. Mark ripped the roots away, taking patches of his skin and hair with them. The pain was intense. Electric.

Soft...the white fuzz promised.

"No," Mark gasped.

Soft...

Mark screamed. It felt like acid was coursing through his veins. Only water would stop the pain. Only water would make it soft.

Soft...

"Get out of my fucking head," he roared. His voice cracked from the strain.

Soft...soft...soft...

"Thirsty..." Mark licked his dry, cracked lips and tasted mold. "No, not thirsty. Hungry. Hungry, you son of a bitch."

More pain greeted this, but Mark did his best to ignore it. Instead, he reached above him and opened the cabinet door. Inside was a Tupperware container half-full of homemade cookies. Paula had baked them the day the rain started, before they'd known it was the end of the world. Now, they were all that was left to remind him of her—to remind him of his humanity. The dampness had taken everything else. Their life together was mildewed and drenched, but the cookies had remained dry, safe inside their airtight container. Paula's homemade cookies and candied apples had been enjoyed by people all across the country. An author friend of theirs had once called her baking skills "divine." When Mark pulled the lid off and smelled them, he smiled, thinking of his wife.

Soft...soft...soft...

Pain ripped through his head. His skin itched and burned. Despite his severe dehydration, his mouth watered.

SOFT...SOFT...SOFT...

His stomach grumbled, and as he reached inside the container and pulled out a cookie, Mark wished he had something to drink with it. A cold glass of milk or a bottle of beer or some...

Water. Cold, clear water.

Soft...

Yes, some water would be perfect. It would be...soft.

Soft...

"No!" Mark crammed the entire cookie in his mouth, clamping his jaws shut and chewing fast. He moaned with delight, feeling his humanity come rushing back, no matter how temporarily. His lips smacked together in contentment. Cookie crumbs clung to his stubble and to the fungus, as well.

The pain intensified. Clutching his abdomen, Mark bent over. Cramps raced through him. His muscles were knots of agony. He balled his hands into fists, tight enough that his fingernails cut into his fuzz-covered palms. Long, thin ropes of saliva dripped from his panting mouth. The fungus didn't like this. Oh, no. The fungus wanted him to die—to liquefy. It needed water to chemically break his body down. Food halted that effect. Food was poison to the white fuzz. Mark didn't know how he knew this, but he did. Perhaps it was some weird symbiosis—a shared consciousness between his mind and the thing that had invaded it.

Paula's cookies were all that was left of everything that had been good and right with the world, and they were his only weapons against the fungus. Cringing as another jolt shot through him, Mark reached for the container.

Soft...*Soft*...*Soft*...

"Fuck you. Have another one."

SOFT...*SOFT*...*SO*—

"FUCK YOU!"

He crammed another cookie into his mouth, doing his best to swallow it whole. The pain became crippling. Mark screamed. Inside his head, the fungus screamed along with him. He grabbed another cookie. A spasm shot through him, and his fist clenched, crushing the cookie. Crumbs fell to the floor, floating atop the water. Mark followed them, collapsing in the throes of a seizure. Smiling through the pain, Mark closed his eyes. He died with the taste of his wife's cookies on his tongue.

SERENADE

The Jet Ski's motor cut out as Don Koish swerved around some floating debris. Gritting his teeth, Don got it going again. The needle on the gas gauge was well past the empty mark. As he bounced up over the crest of a wave, the engine sputtered, then smoked, and finally died.

"Oh great," Don shouted. "That's just fucking wonderful!"

Overhead, seabirds circled him, squawking their delight— hoping he'd give up so that they could feast. Don tried starting the Jet Ski again, but it was pointless. He was out of gas— dead on the water.

"What else can go wrong?"

The Jet Ski tipped over, spilling him into the ocean. Don gasped, plunging beneath the waves. Cold, foul water closed over his head, full of the drifting remnants of a lost civilization. Something bumped into him. He opened his eyes and saw that it was a decapitated head. Fish had eaten the lips, nose and eyes. The white flesh floated around the skull in barely-tethered ribbons. Don screamed, and water rushed down his throat.

For a brief second, he saw movement below him, farther down in the depths. Then his vision blurred from lack of oxygen, and the shadowy form was gone. He kicked for the surface and emerged again above the waves, coughing and gagging. Already, the swift current had carried the Jet Ski away, and he had to hurry to catch up with it. Don was a strong swimmer. Everyone is his family had been. Living in Escanaba, Michigan, only about six blocks from Lake Michigan, they didn't really have a choice. That was what he was swimming in now—the combined volume of the lake,

127

along with all the other rivers and streams—not to mention the falling rain. But considering the depths below him, it had to be more than that. There was just too much water. A survivor had told him that the Atlantic Ocean had rolled right over the Mid-Atlantic states and come as far as Michigan, but Don didn't know if he believed that. Besides, the man who'd told him that had been crazy. He'd also said there were giant, man-eating worms crawling around some of the higher elevations that were still above water. That was ridiculous. Then again, if someone had told him a year ago that Escanaba and the rest of Michigan would be underwater, Don would have said that sounded ridiculous, as well.

Once he'd reached the Jet Ski, Don tried to flip it upright again, and found that he couldn't. He was too weak. Before the rains had started, Don had been an imposing figure. He was built like a refrigerator and his shaved head made him look like a club bouncer or mob muscle. He dug the look and the effect it had on people when they first met him. But now he was thinner. His flesh was pale and sallow, and his tattered clothes hung from him like rags. What little food he'd had left was gone now. His gym bag had tumbled into the ocean when the Jet Ski fell over. Inside had been his cigarette lighters, first aid kit, weapons, and everything else that had kept him alive so far. Also gone were Don's pictures of his wife, Debbie, and their kids.

Dead in the water, he thought again. *What's the fucking point, anymore?*

A particularly strong wave slapped him in the face. Clinging to the Jet Ski, Don put his head down and caught his breath. His throat was sore from coughing, and his mouth tasted oily. He wondered what else was in the water besides the severed head. Probably all kinds of chemicals and shit. His stomach cramped, and he vomited water again. Exhausted, he floated on the tide, shivering as the night grew darker. There was no moon; the cloud cover was too thick. Waves lapped at him and raindrops pelted his arms and head. Thunder rumbled overhead.

Don began to cry. His tears fell like the rain. What was

the point of all this? He was miserable. Why was he trying so hard to go on, to survive? Debbie and the kids were gone. His parents were gone. His friends and co-workers. Their house. His books. Everything he held dear was already beneath the waves. Why didn't he just let go of the Jet Ski and join them below? Just end it all—end his constant, pervasive suffering. End his hunger and thirst. End his pains, both physical and emotional. Why go on living when life sucked so fucking bad?

He looked up at the sky and all he saw was rain. Don took a deep breath. He was about to let go of the Jet Ski and slip beneath the surface, when he heard singing. A woman's voice drifted across the waves, beautiful and melodious—and just a little bit sad. Don couldn't understand the words, but he felt them. As he listened, his grief and self-pity disappeared. He forgot about his family. The voice made him feel good. It had a calming, hypnotic effect. Mesmerized, he glanced around, searching for the source.

Then, he saw her in the darkness. A woman floated a few yards away. Even though it was night, she seemed to shine with a luminescence all her own. Her hips and legs were beneath the surface, but she was naked from the waist up. Long, black hair cascaded down her back and shoulders, stopping at her large, round breasts. She was beautiful. Don's breath caught in his throat. As she sang, the woman stared right at him. Even with the mist and rain and distance between them, Don could see her eyes clearly. It felt like they were looking right through him. He cocked his head to one side, entranced. The woman smiled.

"Hey," he called, "are you okay?"

Her only response was to continue singing. The melody echoed over the roar of the surf. The current carried her closer. Her milky skin glistened with droplets of water. She raised one hand and beckoned to him. Despite the fact that he'd been immersed in cold water, his penis stirred.

The song called to him. Without thinking, Don let go of the Jet Ski and swam towards her. His throbbing erection strained against his zipper. He kicked harder, pushing himself against the current, heedless of his exhausted state. The song got louder. He felt the melody picking through his brain—invisible fingers, poking and prodding, trying to control him. He surrendered willingly.

They embraced, arms entwining, eyes closed. Then Don stopped her song with a kiss. Her breasts pressed against his chest as they kissed. He took her wet hair in his hands. They continued kissing, and he ran his fingertips down her back, then her hips, and finally slipped them beneath the surface.

Don froze. His eyes shot open. The woman was smiling again, and this time, he saw how sharp her teeth were. Like a shark's. She pressed on Don's shoulders and shoved him beneath the surface. The last thing he saw before drowning was her lower half. Instead of legs, the woman had a grayish-silver fish tail, all covered with scales.

She took him deeper into the depths with a final kiss.

Quiet returned to the ocean's surface, disturbed only by the rain.

THE FINAL PRINCIPLE

Boston, Massachusetts

Hell wasn't hot and dry. It was cold and wet.

Steven Kazmirski and his wife, Nahed Shahabi, rowed in darkness across the open water, afraid to use the boat's motor or spotlight. Both might attract predators. There was no sound, except for the falling rain and the waves lapping against the side of their craft. Tonight, even the gulls were quiet. Occasionally, dead bodies bumped against their oars. The stillness was overwhelming.

Rain seeped through their lifejackets and clothing. Steven shivered in the cold, and wondered again if they'd done the right thing leaving their shelter on the John Hancock Tower. Especially with Nahed being pregnant. Maybe they'd have been better off staying in California. Of course, California was underwater, too. They'd lived there when Steven was a post-doc at UC Berkeley. Then they'd moved across the country to Newton and bought half of a two-family home. That house, built in 1912, had withstood a lot—wars, economic depressions, civil unrest. But it couldn't hold up against the weather. Steven got a job at a major pharmaceutical company in Cambridge, just across the Charles River from Boston. He solved protein structures with potential drug compounds. Nahed attended film school for documentary filmmaking. Life was good.

Then the rains came.

As far as they knew, they were the last people left alive in what had once been Boston. Well, almost. Like many other survivors, they'd listened to Mark Sylva's pirate radio broadcasts from atop the Prudential Building, simultaneously enthralled and repelled by Sylva's day-by-day commentary on how the white fuzz had claimed his companions, and finally himself. The last communication was twelve hours ago. The radio had played nothing but static since.

Steven glanced back at his wife. His heart ached. By her expression, it was obvious she was thinking about the baby. Burman, their Himalayan cat, was curled up beneath Nahed's seat, cold and wet and miserable. Burman thought himself bigger and meaner than he actually was, and was really clumsy. The weather had not improved his mood, but there was no way they could leave him behind. Steven had tried—urged them both to stay put while he went to the Prudential Building. But Nahed insisted. They were in this together, as a family.

He only wished the boat had washed up on the tower sooner, so he could have helped Sylva and his friends before the disease had progressed too far. Listening to it happen, hearing the man's sanity crumble and his humanity slip away, and being unable to do anything about it had been tough. Going into the belly of the beast with his pregnant wife and their cat was even harder.

They drifted through the fog in silence. Steven worried that they might miss the building and head farther out to sea, away from any possibility of shelter. Then the mist parted and the Pru' loomed before them. Once, it had towered almost eight hundred feet above the city. Now, only the top three floors stuck out above the ocean, along with the two hundred foot radio tower on the roof. Steven flipped wet hair out of his eyes. His grip tightened around the oar.

"Are you sure about this?" Nahed asked.

He nodded. "With my biochemistry and drug development background? I've got to do this. If I can learn more about how it spreads, then—"

Nahed interrupted. "But what if you get infected? I don't want to have our baby alone."

He stopped rowing and squeezed her knee. Burman growled at the disturbance.

"I'm doing this for our baby. And for you. For all we know, I might be the last person left on Earth who can stop this."

"Can you stop the rain, as well?"

"Let's focus on one thing at a time."

Steven's plan was simple—at least to him. He didn't know yet if the white fuzz was fungal, alien or bacterial, but it was certainly alive, and therefore contained different proteins. If he could obtain a pure sample of a protein that was essential in the machinery that replicated the white fuzz's DNA, then he could stop it with drugs. If the DNA couldn't replicate, the white fuzz couldn't grow. He intended to collect fungus samples and extract the protein using gravity and chromatography columns. Then he'd add the drug—either a small chemical molecule or a bio-molecule that had been purified. Once he'd gotten the drug complex to crystallize, he could have a potential cure within a week.

He'd explained all this to Nahed. What he hadn't told her was that he'd also need an X-ray generator. So after they obtained the sample, they'd need to find a major university, pharmaceutical company, or government lab that wasn't underwater. He'd heard that the Havenbrook facility in Pennsylvania was still functioning and intended to try for that. Steven also needed power to run the X-ray generator and the computers for the math and structure viewing. If Havenbrook was without electricity, he could always rig up some gas generators.

And then he could save the world.

Although he'd never admit it to himself, Steven knew deep down inside that his plan would never work. But he couldn't just sit by and do nothing. He had a baby on the way. He needed to make the world a better place. Needed to be a father. Needed to feel like he was doing everything possible to ensure his family's protection—to make the world a safer place for his child.

They pulled alongside the building. Steven shattered a window and peeked inside, seeing a corridor. He picked the broken glass out of the way and crawled through. Nahed handed him the cat, and then followed. The three of them huddled together in the dark, musty hallway. Rain pooled at their feet. Steven un-holstered his pistol. He'd become a very good shot since the world ended; he had plenty of time to practice target shooting. With his other hand, he shined a flashlight around. The walls and ceiling were covered with mildew. Water dripped steadily through cracked plaster. Steven saw no signs of the white fuzz.

"If we find some," he whispered. "I want you to stay back. Whatever you do, don't touch it."

"I promise," Nahed said. "But the same goes for you."

They proceeded down the hallway. Burman darted ahead, tail twitching, and vanished into the shadows.

"Burman!" Nahed's voice echoed down the corridor.

The cat hissed at something. Gripping each other's hands, Steven and Nahed crept forward. In the darkness, Burman spat. Then his growls turned to fearful whines. He jumped out of the shadows, ran between their legs and hid behind them.

Something else followed him. Something inhuman. A figure lurched from the darkness, its body covered in white fuzz. There was no face left—just an empty hole to serve as a mouth and two black dots that might have been eyes. Root-like tendrils hung off its arms and legs. It stumbled towards them slowly, reeking of mildew. Nahed screamed. Steven raised the pistol.

The creature spoke. "Alex...*soft*...need...*soft*..."

Alex. Steven remembered that Sylva had talked about his son. The boy's name was Alex. He waved the gun at the shambling fungus.

"Mr. Sylva?" His voice cracked. "Mr. Mark Sylva?"

"Me...*soft*...kill...*soft*...me...*soft*...turning into...*soft*...water..."

"My God," Steven breathed. "It's okay. We're here to help you."

"Kill...*soft*...me...*soft*...wants...*soft*...to...*soft*...kill...*soft*...you..."

The creature's tone changed. Moving with sudden swiftness, it lunged at them, arms outstretched. The pistol jumped in Steven's hand. Once. Twice. Three times. Brass casings bounced off the walls. Sylva toppled over and exploded, gushing all over the floor. Nahed and Steven jumped backward as the infected man's body turned to water. The puddle spread, filling the hallway.

"Back to the window," Steven shouted. "Hold your breath. Don't inhale!"

They grabbed Burman and jumped back into the boat. The rain seemed louder. It wasn't until they were back at the John Hancock Tower that Steven began to tremble. Sobs racked his body. Nahed took him in her arms.

"You don't have to save the world," she said, kissing his tears away. "You don't have to be a hero. You are my husband and the father of our child. That is more important than anything else."

She put his hands on her belly. Burman curled up between them and began licking himself. The four of them sat there, listening to the rain, and eventually, they fell asleep.

LIQUID NOOSE

Somewhere in the New Pacific

The yacht rocked gently on the tide. Paul Legerski leaned against the rail and gazed out at the ocean. The flotsam and jetsam from the remains of southern California was finally clearing, and the surface was less polluted now, but shrouded in mist. He could see about seventy feet. After that, the world just disappeared. Paul thought of the old sailors who cruised the seas before it was common knowledge that the Earth was round. They'd worried about falling off the edge of the world. He imagined that he now knew how they felt. He was clinging to the edge of the world, perilously close to slipping off.

Paul's fingers tightened around the wet handrail. Rain dripped from his nose and chin.

"You know," he said, "if all of this water would freeze over, maybe it wouldn't be such a bad thing."

The four men said nothing. Even if they'd wanted to respond, they couldn't have. Paul had gagged all four of them when he tied their hands and feet together behind their backs.

Smiling, Paul continued. "Imagine it—the world's biggest fucking ice hockey rink. Shit, the world as an ice hockey rink! Watch the San Jose Sharks play against the Mighty Ducks. One goal above the United States and the other team's goal somewhere over Europe. Pretty fucking sweet, right?"

One of the men snorted through his nose, dripping blood and snot all over the duct tape covering his mouth. His eyes shone with hate. His clothes were soaked. All of them were. Paul had left them lying here in the rain.

"Not a hockey fan?" Paul asked. "I am. I used to be a goaltender. Used to watch the Sharks practice all the time. I love hockey." Pausing, he glanced back out at the ocean. His

136

fingers tightened around the rail. "Shannon was a big hockey fan, too."

Above them, a circling flock of seagulls shrieked.

Paul spun around and backhanded the glaring man. The blow made a sound like a snapping tree branch. The other three men jumped, startled. The prisoner's head rocked back. His eyes were wide. Veins stood out in his neck and forehead, and there was a red handprint on his cheek. Paul's hand stung. Wincing, he rubbed it with his other hand. The pain felt good.

"Did you slap my wife like that? Huh? Did you fuckers beat her before you raped her?"

Above them, the birds grew louder.

"Shannon and I were married on a yacht," Paul said. "Just like this one."

One of the prisoners began to cry. He tried to speak around the duct tape, but his words were garbled.

"Save it," Paul said. "You fucks took her from me. Now you're going to pay."

When the flooding started, Paul and Shannon had been rescued, along with some other survivors from Corona, by the National Guard. They'd been transported to a shelter, but that was soon flooded as well. They'd ended up floating in a derelict fishing boat, along with three Mexicans who'd been stranded on a rooftop. One by one, their companions had died. Two of them got sick—infected by some kind of white fungus that grew over their bodies. Both men had dived into the ocean, screaming for water. The third man had been yanked out of the boat by a long, green tentacle and pulled beneath the surface.

Soon, their fishing boat had started to sink. Paul could swim, but he hated the water. He'd tried to get scuba certified in Hawaii a few years back, but had freaked out once his head went underwater and there was no sound or visibility. The sensory deprivation shook him so badly that he'd popped up from the ocean floor and quit. Shannon had never taken swim lessons, but she could snorkel. Frantic, Paul and Shannon were preparing to abandon it when a yacht came along. They'd thought they were rescued. Instead, the men aboard the yacht had invited them onboard. Then they'd bashed Paul in the head and knocked him unconscious.

When he woke up, Shannon was dead. He saw her naked, bloody body lying on the deck. Saw the men standing over her, pulling up their pants. Saw their firearms within his reach, forgotten by the men.

Then he'd seen nothing but red.

And here they were now.

Whistling, Paul walked into the yacht's galley and rummaged through a Styrofoam ice chest. There was no ice in it, but there were several warm bottles of bourbon, scotch, and tequila. Paul selected one, pulled the cap off, and drank. Again, the pain was good. He walked back out onto the rain-slicked deck, clutching the bottle and singing. The prisoners watched him fearfully.

"All I want from you is another round," Paul sang. "Slamming faster just to hit the ground." He took another swig and then continued. "Tip another glass just to get me loose. Tying on another big liquid noose."

His singing faded. The men squirmed and flopped on the deck. A particularly large swell rocked the boat. Paul kept his balance. When the sea had calmed again, he set down the bottle and picked up the gun and a knife. He stood over the cowering prisoners. His smile was bitter.

"I'm going to give you guys something that you didn't give my wife. A chance. But if you fuck with me, then the deal is off. Understood?"

One of them nodded. The others stared blankly.

Paul knelt in front of the first man and cut the ropes around his ankles. Groaning beneath his duct tape gag, the man stretched his legs. Paul stood up again and backed away, covering the man with the pistol.

"Get up."

The man stumbled to his feet.

"Walk over to the side. Right up against the rail."

Slowly, the man did as ordered.

Paul motioned with the gun. "Now, jump."

The man's eyes grew wide. He looked out over the side

and then back to Paul.

"Jump," Paul repeated. "I freed your legs. If you can get your hands free in time, you might not drown. You might—"

The man lowered his head and charged. Paul squeezed the trigger. The man tumbled to the deck.

"I warned you guys not to fuck with me." Paul shook his head. "I guess we'll go with plan B."

He tossed the dead man's body over the side and watched it sink beneath the waves. Then he tied nooses around each of the remaining men's necks, leaving the ropes loose enough for them to breath. He tied the other end of the ropes to the rail.

"This is for my wife."

One by one, Paul tossed each man over the side, watched the ropes pull tight, and began singing again.

THE CHASE

Phoenix, Arizona

The monsters weren't real, but that didn't stop Philip Harms from shooting them.

"What we've got here," he said, doing his best Cool Hand Luke impression, "is a failure of suspension of disbelief."

Or maybe that was Guns N' Roses. He couldn't remember anymore. His head ached all the time.

He knew he was going crazy. How else to explain this? He'd been holed up on the top floors of the Chase Tower for too long now—starving, no electricity, nothing to do but listen to the rain and cry. That was enough to drive any man insane. And it had; obviously, because the things pouring through the broken windows each time a wave crashed against the building's exterior simply couldn't exist in nature. They were scientific impossibilities—with teeth.

Laughing, he fired another round. A starfish-shaped creature with a human face sagged to the wet floor. Two more took its place. Fiffy, his black and tan Doberman, seized a smaller creature in her jaws and shook it. Philip couldn't tell what it was. It had a tail like a fish but screamed like a child. Growling, Fiffy flung it against the wall.

Philip backed down the hallway. Another wave crashed into the building and the water level rose past his ankles. Gun smoke filled the corridor, along with a fishy, chlorine stench—like a bedroom after sex, but sharper. He wondered how far away they were from the stairwell leading up to the observation deck, but couldn't risk glancing over his shoulder to see. It probably didn't matter anyway. Chances were good he and Fiffy wouldn't survive the night.

The Chase had been the perfect refuge—the only refuge,

really. Situated in a valley, the rest of Phoenix was underwater. There were mountaintops on the horizon, barely visible through the gloom, but he'd had no way to reach them. A few cell phone towers and antennae jutted from the churning waters, but only the Chase Tower remained intact. Philip and Fiffy had occupied the top three floors. The lower floors were flooded. They'd been miserable. Their situation was dire. But they'd still been alive. There was still hope.

Until tonight.

The waters had risen higher. One of the windows shattered. That was all it took. Now, their refuge was flooding, and the water brought nightmares with it. The Chase had become a prison. Philip knew all about prisons. He'd been a Correctional Officer for the Arizona prison system. He'd worked at Lewis Prison in Buckeye during the longest hostage crisis in U.S. history. Those had been dark times. Terrifying.

This was worse.

A massive, green tentacle crashed into the building, and a section of the wall crumbled. Black water rushed in, along with more monsters. A shimmering school of tiny fish launched themselves from the torrent and sailed towards him on wing-like fins. Their gnashing teeth sounded like the buzz of a hummingbird. One of them nipped Fiffy's ear, severing the tip. Yelping, the dog refused to budge, holding her ground.

Philip holstered the pistol and pulled the shotgun off his back. Handguns were no good against such small, moving targets. He squeezed the trigger and thunder filled the hall. Some of the fish fell. The others turned in mid-air and fled.

Philip loathed implausibility. He was reminded of a novel by a writer whom he enjoyed trolling on the internet, in which birds and fish came back as zombies. The author had apparently never seen a dead bird. Birds had essential oils in their feathers which allowed them to fly. A dead bird wouldn't continue producing those oils. Plus, a bird's neck muscle contracted after death. An animal with a twisted neck wouldn't be very aerodynamic. Therefore, dead birds couldn't fly. And the things attacking the building were just like those zombie birds. Sharks with human arms and legs. Giant worms.

141

Flying piranha. Starfish people. Fungal humanoids, covered with something that looked like white peach fuzz. And even a fucking mermaid!

As the shotgun jerked in his hands, Philip wondered if the attackers were imaginary. Then he glanced at his wounded dog and decided they weren't. After all, Fiffy could see them, too.

"*Soft...*" one of the fungus creatures warbled in an all-too-human voice. It sounded like it was gargling.

"I'm anything but soft, friend."

He shot it in the head, and then tossed the shotgun aside. He had no more shells for it. He was down to the Glock 19, the Walther PPK, and the Makarov .380 ACP. Wishing for an AR-15, Philip pulled the Walther from its holster and resumed fire, still inching towards the stairwell. The monsters never slowed. Grinning, he wished they were inmates. He knew what an imposing figure he'd been at the prison. Philip was almost six feet tall and weighed two hundred and fifty-five pounds. His brown hair was cropped into a flattop. He was still wearing his uniform, although it was now tattered and dirty—brown BDU pants, tan shirt, and military-style boots. Topping off the ensemble were his mirrored sunglasses. His seven-pointed star badge was still pinned to his shirt.

Apparently, none of this impressed the creatures. They kept swarming down the corridor in wave after wave, clambering over the corpses of their fallen comrades. The water rose to his knees, and up to Fiffy's neck. A long, thin worm slithered through the water on the floor and reared to strike. Fiffy seized it. Another one crawled up Philip's leg. He blasted it in half. Ichor splattered his clothing and dripped from his goatee.

Reaching the stairwell, Philip and Fiffy ran up to the observation deck. Access to the deck had been shut off after 9/11, but Philip had forced the doors open weeks ago, so that he and Fiffy could get fresh air and drinking water, as well as birds for dinner. They ran out onto the roof and Philip slammed the door shut behind them, glancing around for something to block it with. Fiffy barked at the sky. Ignoring her, he grabbed a heavy trashcan and dragged it over to the doorway. It wouldn't hold long, but with luck, it would slow their pursuers down long enough for him and Fiffy to take up defensive positions.

Fiffy's barks turned to whines, low and mournful.

Philip turned to her. "What's wrong, girl? What do you—"

The rain stopped. Philip stared upward and realized why. The biggest impossibility of all loomed over them, dwarfing the building. It was hard for him to make out all of the details because much of it was swallowed up in the gloom. It had a bulbous head with multiple tentacles, and its flesh looked gelatinous. Two monstrous eyes, the size of school buses, glared at him with a malevolent intelligence. The creature's towering bulk blocked out the rain.

Fiffy howled.

Philip barely had time to scream before his disbelief was squashed forever.

ONE LAST BREATH

Saint Louis, Missouri

Rain blasted down like liquid bullets and the water continued to rise. The Mississippi River and all of the nearby lakes, ponds, and reservoirs had joined forces to create a torrid new ocean. The land was flatter than a pancake, and natural elevation was hard to find. The Cahokia Indian burial mounds, located in the Mississippi flood plain, were underwater. So were the Shawnee National Forest and all but the tips of the Shawnee Hills. The highest points were manmade.

Roman Wuller and his five-year old son, Dashiell, had taken shelter on the top floor of the forty-five story tall US Bank building, where Roman had worked until the end of the world. The building was deserted except for the two of them—and a few dead people, their corpses covered in white fungus, liquefying where they lay. Roman had seen a few other survivors pass by in boats, and a small group that had huddled together atop the St. Louis arch, until something beneath the waves had pulled them under with its tentacles. None of them had resurfaced.

Roman and Dashiell hadn't gone outside much after that.

Now they had no choice.

The waters had finally crept onto their floor, slowly filling the rooms and hallways. Roman had bundled Dashiell up tight against the weather, and made him put on the one life vest they had. Then the two of them had retreated up to the roof. At first, Dashiell had refused to leave, so Roman had to challenge him to a race up the stairs to motivate him. The water followed them up the stairwell, step by step.

They stood in the center of the roof. Roman watched the ocean's surface, searching for movement—the tentacles of a lurking predator, or more hopefully, a passing boat or raft. The horizons were deserted.

Dashiell clutched the big, black stuffed dog that his grandfather had bought him. It was soaked through, but he held it tight. Roman hoisted the boy above his shoulders—one last piggyback ride before the inevitable. Waves lapped against the sides of the building, and water seeped from beneath the service door leading down into the flooded floors below. The rain pelted them like tears, and Roman tried not to cry. He thought of his wife, Judy, and his daughters, Shannon and Allison—gone now, washed away in the flood.

Another wave crashed into the building and swamped the roof. The water reached Roman's ankles. Shuffling his feet, he readjusted his grip on his son's legs. Dashiell was tall and thin for his age. Roman's shoulders ached, but he ignored the pain. He glanced up at his son, blinking against the rain. Dashiell stared down at him, blonde hair plastered to his head, blue eyes saddened and afraid. His beautiful smile was non-existent. Roman missed it.

"I need you to be brave for me, okay?"

Dashiell nodded. "Sure."

That was always his response when asked to do something, and his two older sisters had often taken advantage of that. Roman choked back tears. The water lapped at his knees.

"You've got your life vest on. It will help you float. When I let go of you—"

"No, Dad! Don't let go!"

Roman shushed him, and then continued. "The water is getting higher. I'm going to hold you up above it. When I let go, I want you to swim."

"I can't."

"The life vest will do most of the work. And you're a good swimmer."

"So are you, Daddy."

"Yeah," Roman's voice cracked. "I sure am."

But how long can I float, he thought. *How long?*

Roman was an avid swimmer and was certified in scuba diving, but they only had the one life vest. He couldn't float forever. The better question was how long could he hold his breath? Ninety seconds? Two minutes. The answer was as long as it took—as long as Dashiell stayed safe, above the waves. The water reached Roman's waist. He shivered, trying not to let Dashiell see how scared he was.

"We're buddies, right, Daddy?" His voice sounded unsure and afraid.

"Sure we are."

"And that won't change, right?" Dashiell abhorred change.

"That will never change, Dashiell. I'll always love you."

"What's going to happen, Dad? Are you going to go away like Grandpa?"

The water surged around Roman's belly button and his heart broke. Dashiell had a big heart and had loved his grandfather. The two had been very close. It wasn't until after he'd passed away that Roman had come to appreciate how much his parents had done for him. Now, all he had were memories—but that was enough.

For a little while longer.

"Dashiell, do you remember watching Speed Racer with me?"

"Yeah, Dad. It's your favorite. And Johnny Quest and Tobor the Eighth Man. Don't you know that Tobor is Robot spelled backwards? Just like in my kindergarten books."

"That's right." Roman blinked tears away. The water reached his chest. "And remember helping me in the yard, raking leaves. And watching your sisters play volleyball. Hitting tennis balls over the roof and how I always got them out of the gutter for you. Riding your scooter. And how you left me and Mommy little notes with your Post-It pads. And how you'd climb in bed with us because you thought your bed was too big."

"I remember."

"I need you to be brave now. Pretty soon, I'm going to have to hold my breath. When I let go of you, be brave and swim away, just like I've taught you."

"But my dog—"

"You'll be able to hold onto him. Remember, you've got

your life vest."

"But what about you, Daddy?"

"We only have the one life vest, so I'm going to hold you up above the water and then hold my breath."

"For how long?"

Roman smiled as the water reached his chin. "For as long as I have to."

Thunder boomed overhead, and the sky crackled with lightning. Another wave roared towards them.

"I love you, Dashiell. I'm very proud of you, and I love you. Remember that, too, okay?"

"Daddy?" Dashiell squeezed his legs together and gripped his father's head. "What's going to happen?"

"Just be brave. And remember that I love you. Okay?"

"I love you, too, Daddy."

Roman took several quick breaths. Then he sucked in a deep lungful of air and the water closed over his nose and mouth.

I can do this, he thought. *As long as it takes. Just hold him above water until the life vest does the rest.*

The water closed over his ears and eyes, and the world changed. He saw nothing but darkness, and sounds became muted. The rain was distant static. The crashing waves and thunder were echoes from far away. Roman started to count.

One Mississippi...

Two Mississippi...

Three Mississippi...

At sixty, his pulse throbbed in his ears and throat and his chest ached.

I love you, Dashiell. Remember...

At one hundred and twenty seconds, his lungs felt like they were on fire, and there were white spots in the darkness around him. Roman had been raised Catholic. He wasn't sure what he believed, but in his last moments, he prayed that God would watch over his son and keep him safe. Then he continued counting.

Remember, Dashiell...

The white spots coalesced, forming figures. Roman saw

his parents and Judy and the girls. He wondered dimly if Dashiell could see them as well. His family smiled at him. The pain in his lungs eased, and Roman felt calm and peaceful.

Two hundred and forty...

Two hundred and forty one...

Two hundred and forty two...

Remember...

Two hundred and for...

Dashiell floated away. Roman felt the weight leave his shoulders. He closed his eyes and took a deep breath.

THE LAST
GHOST OF MARY

Somewhere in the New Pacific

"Joann?"

He'd thought he heard her voice on the wind, calling him.
"Damn seagulls…"

Jamie La Chance was close to death. He welcomed it.
Wished it would hurry along, end his suffering, and silence the
incessant, droning rain. He'd had a nice, comfortable home
that he shared with his wife, Joann. One of the extra bedrooms
had been filled with pictures of Jamie and his favorite authors,
and various pieces of original horror artwork. All gone now,
submerged with the rest of Rowland Heights. Their home had
been warm and dry. They'd never wanted for food or water or
anything else.

Now Jamie floated on a powerless Yamaha wave runner,
its four-cycle engine as dead as the rest of the world. He was
out of gas and out of time. His last meal had been seven days
ago; he'd found a dead fish floating on the tide, and devoured
it raw. Even though it hadn't been infected with the strange,
white fungus he'd seen growing on other fish, it still made him
sick. There was no shortage of water, of course. He caught
rain in an empty soup can, but it tasted oily and bitter. Jamie
wished for a bottle of clear, cold spring water. That would ease
his fever.

He missed Joann, and their kids, Travis and Leslie, and
their families. There was a chance that Leslie and her husband,
Martin, might still be alive. They lived in Nampa, Idaho,
which had a higher elevation. Maybe the floodwaters hadn't
reached them yet.

He hoped he'd see Joann soon.

And then he saw something else.

It floated out of the mist, sails fluttering in the breeze—a brigantine like the kind that had sailed in the late 1800's. Jamie knew a lot about boats and ships, and guessed its weight at close to three hundred tons, and its length at just over one hundred feet. The decks were deserted. Nothing moved onboard the vessel. Seagulls hovered around its masts, their bodies covered with the same white fungus he'd seen growing on the fish. The ship bore down on him, moving fast. As it got closer, he heard the boards creaking.

"Shit." Jamie licked his cracked lips and tried to shout. "Hello! Anybody there?"

His voice was hoarse and weak.

The brigantine's passing stirred the surface. The waves grew choppier and the Yamaha bobbed up and down, threatening to capsize. Jamie surveyed the decks, but saw no one. If the crew was onboard, they were below decks. The ship pulled alongside him and Jamie mustered the last of his strength. He reached out and grabbed a dangling rope, clinging to it as he was lifted off the wave runner and dragged along the ocean's surface.

Sputtering and trying to keep his head above water, Jamie hauled himself up the rope. His muscles ached and his arms and legs trembled. As he neared the rail, Jamie spotted the ship's name, engraved in the wood near the bow.

MARY CELESTE

Jamie shivered and it had nothing to do with his fever or the rain. He knew that name. The Mary Celeste was the archetypal ghost ship and one of the most famous nautical legends of all time. It was found unmanned and under full sail in the Atlantic Ocean in 1872. A group of sailors who boarded her found the ship in good condition, but soaked. Reports at the time had described it as "a thoroughly wet mess." There was water between decks and in the hold. The fore hatch and lazarette were both open, the clock was not functioning, and the compass had been destroyed. The fate of the crew was unknown. The ship's only lifeboat was missing, as were the sextant and the marine chronometer. The captain's log gave no indication of distress or trouble. Most bizarre was what they discovered in the galley—untouched breakfasts congealing on plates with full cups of tea and silverware on the side. It was as if the crew had vanished right before eating. The boarding party debarked and the ship vanished across the horizon. In the years since, the Mary Celeste had been sighted hundreds of times all over the world. The ghost ship sailed the Atlantic, Pacific, and Indian Oceans, as well as the Mediterranean and North Seas. Many sailors believed that when the Mary Celeste crossed their bow, it was an omen of impending doom. Legend had it that the crewless vessel would cruise the sea until it reached the end of the world.

Jaime heaved himself over the rail and tumbled to the deck with a thud. He lay on his back on the wet boards, gasping for breath. He closed his eyes against the rain drops pelting his face. After a few moments, he opened them again and struggled to his feet.

"Hello," he called, "is there anyone here?"

There was no answer—just more of that unnerving creaking. He tried to shout, but the wind seemed to snatch his voice away.

"I need help. I'm sick…dying! Anyone?"

The ship was deserted, just like in the old tales.

A powerful swell struck the hull and the ship listed to one side. Jamie stumbled, struggling to keep his balance. His feet slipped on the wet deck and he slid into the rail. Panicked, he gripped the rail tightly as the ship rolled even further. Then, slowly, it righted itself again. As the vertigo passed, Jaime glanced down at the ocean. The wave runner was receding as the Mary Celeste raced on into the storm.

He wiped the rain from his eyes and stared. There was a figure clinging to the wave runner.

"Who is that?"

Lightning flashed overhead, lighting up the ocean. Realization crept over him. He'd been wrong. The figure wasn't clinging to the wave runner. It was limp. Dead.

The body was his.

The ghost ship sailed on, speeding towards the end of the world.

AT THE MOUNTAINS OF MELTING

Drammen, Oslo, Norway

The mountains were melting. Trygve Botnen was sure of it. At first, he'd thought it was some sort of bizarre mirage, a visual effect brought on by the extreme weather or his sheer exhaustion and hunger. It occurred to him that maybe hypothermia was finally settling in. He'd tried his best to ignore what he was seeing, but there was no denying it anymore. The very ground beneath his feet was liquefying. Soon, there'd be nothing left for him to stand on.

If the snow worms didn't get him first.

The ground began to tremble again. The earthquakes had only started a few days ago, but they kept increasing in both frequency and intensity. At first, he'd thought they were aftershocks from the initial quake. He remained still until the shaking ceased. Despite his heavy layers of clothing, Trygve shivered. Then he trudged on, wading through the snow and keeping an eye out for the worms.

When the flooding began, and the Drammen River overflowed its banks, submerging everything all the way down to the Svelvikstrømmen, Trygve had packed up some supplies and weapons and left civilization behind. By then, he'd seen the news reports from all across the world. Non-stop rain, tsunamis, hurricanes—the devastation was global. Civilization collapsed. Looting and murder were widespread. The worms came next, forced up out of the ground by all the flooding. The last few reports he'd seen before the broadcasts stopped had been full of speculation. The worms weren't included in the fossil record. Perhaps they hadn't been underground at all. Maybe they'd come from somewhere else.

None of it mattered to him. His plan had been simple—

152

make a wilderness walk up Kjøsterudjuvet. Trygve wanted to get high up into the mountains, where there was snow all year, and hide out until things returned to normal. He'd traveled all over the world, including forty-six different states in the U.S., and had hiked in the Himalayas, so mountain climbing was no challenge to him. He figured that the worms wouldn't be able to reach him that high, for the terrain was rocky and frozen and covered with ice and snow. He'd be safe from the worms there.

But he hadn't been.

He'd been right about the weather. While the rest of the world dealt with torrential rain, Trygve suffered through an endless snowstorm. Everywhere he looked, he saw an unbroken, featureless blanket of white. Snow covered everything, making it impossible to see more than a few feet, and extremely difficult to travel. It also made him easy prey for the snow worms.

He'd first seen them when he was still in the lowlands, outside the world-famous Spiral Tunnel. Other survivors had gathered there, all with the same idea as Trygve's. After some discussion, they began to look at Trygve as the leader. He was used to that. As the Vice President of ABN AMRO Asset Management's real estate division, Trygve was used to assuming leadership roles and making command decisions.

They'd been ready to depart as a group, when the worms attacked. They'd come at the survivors from all sides, burrowing under the snow like cartoon gophers, leaving long furrows on top of the surface. At first, none of Trygve's companions had been sure what was happening. Then, an American tourist started gasping. The rest of the group turned their attention to her. Trygve had noticed that one of the furrows ended at her feet. She stood knee-deep in the snow, completely still, as if frozen. Her expression was shocked, yet she made no sound. As they watched, the color drained from her face. She turned pale, then alabaster. Another man tried to assist her, and the woman toppled over in the snow. The ground beneath her feet was red. A long, white worm, about the thickness of a fire hose, was attached to her back. The group screamed in unison, and the worm released the tourist. Half its length was hidden in the snow bank. The rest raised into the air, weaving back and forth. The woman's blood dripped from its yawning mouth.

Another victim was suddenly jerked beneath the snow. Then another. One by one, the group was slaughtered. Trygve managed to escape, killing two of the creatures in the process, but the other refugees were slaughtered. Rather than chasing Trygve, the worms gorged themselves on their victims. The falling snow blanketed the bloodstains.

Trygve made it into the mountains, but the worms had trailed him the whole way. He'd lost count of how many he'd killed since fleeing the Spiral Tunnel. He'd thought that once he reached the higher elevations, they wouldn't follow. He'd been wrong. Somehow, they'd been able to tunnel through solid rock and frozen ground, tracking his every step.

But the worms weren't what concerned him now. Because the way things were going, there wouldn't be any mountains left for the worms to tunnel beneath for very much longer. There wouldn't be anything.

The wind howled around him, lashing at his exposed cheeks and nose like a razor-edged whip. It hurt to breathe. Each time he inhaled, the frigid air made his lungs and head ache. Trygve wanted to lie down in the snow, bury himself beneath it, and just go to sleep.

The mountains were getting shorter. He was sure of it now. The topmost peak was closer to the ground than it had been the day before. Somewhere, deep beneath his feet, the Earth's very foundations were melting away—turning to water. It sounded impossible, but there was no other way to explain the events he was witnessing—the frequent earthquakes, the sinking mountains, the fact that even though the snow didn't stop falling, it didn't seem to be getting higher anymore. Perhaps the most disconcerting part was watching the mountains drift slowly, as if they were floating on the sea.

Another tremor rocked the landscape. Trygve halted, standing with his feet spaced wide apart so that he could keep his balance. A nearby tree crashed to the ground, sending a plume of powdery snow into the air. He heard a distant rumbling from far overhead. An avalanche. He glanced up at the mountain peak. He could no longer see it. It was obscured by a shifting cloud of snow, dust, and rock. As the cloud neared him, the rumbling grew louder. He glanced around, seeking shelter, but instead, he saw the all-too-familiar snow funnels closing in on him.

"Come on," he shouted. "Come on and take me, if you can!"

The worms slithered closer, their bodies still hidden beneath the snow. The rumbling eclipsed all other sounds now, and as it drew closer, Trygve closed his eyes. The avalanche cascaded over them, burying all in a mound of white.

Within hours, that mound began to sink.

EXODUS A. D. (LOCKE'S ARK REPRISE)

Saint Louis, Missouri

It wasn't the first end of the world, nor would it be the last. There had been many throughout time. The apocalypse didn't always involve the end of the physical world. Sometimes in history, it simply heralded bad times for certain groups of people or civilizations—a personal apocalypse.

For the Israelites, the first apocalypse arrived around 1550 B.C., when they were slaves of the Egyptian people. The ruling Pharaoh decreed that all newborn Hebrew males were to be killed. One young mother hid her baby in an ark made of bulrushes and set him adrift in the river, so that her son would escape the slaughter. He floated downstream, and eventually came to rest on the shore. It began to rain. The Pharaoh's daughter found the child and took pity on him, and named the baby Moses, which meant "to take out of the water."

Moses grew up and saved the Israelites from the apocalypse. Their people would face other apocalypses throughout history, but that was the first, and Moses delivered them as he himself was delivered from the water.

Dashiell Wuller didn't know any of this, of course. All he knew was fear and loneliness and discomfort. More than these, he felt a deep, aching sadness. He bobbed on the ocean's surface, not in an ark made of reeds but in a fluorescent orange life vest. He didn't know how long he'd been floating. At age five, Dashiell's sense of time revolved around meals, sleep, and when his favorite cartoons came on. He could recite the days of the week and the numbers on a clock, but couldn't

156

conceptualize tomorrow or next week. All he knew was that he'd been out here a long time. He was wet and cold and terrified, and his legs were starting to feel numb. His lips and teeth hurt from chattering. He clutched his stuffed dog to his chest and tried very hard not to cry.

Lightning split the sky and thunder rumbled. Dashiell shivered. Tears flowed. His Daddy had held him up above the water. He'd stayed like that for a long time, even after the water closed over his head. Then Dashiell felt his father's hands slip away and Dashiell drifted off on the crest of a wave.

There were things in the water. He'd seen them emerge farther away—snaky things that wriggled and splashed, and a bunch of silver fish that jumped out of the water and flew through the air with buzzing wings.

Dashiell missed his family, but he missed his father most of all. He wished his Daddy was here right now, to protect him from the snaky things. He had a feeling they might be bad. He remembered his promise to his father—to be brave. The rain kept falling. He wanted to close his eyes, but every time he did, Dashiell got even more scared. Back home, he and his sisters had played a game called "Mummy." It involved tagging the other players while jumping on a trampoline. Each time a new kid came over to play, his sisters would explain that Dashiell was out of bounds to be tagged because he was too scared to be the mummy. The mummy had to keep their eyes closed and their arms straight out, trying to tag one of the others on the trampoline. Bobbing up and down in the water had the same effect, so he kept his eyes open and clung to his stuffed dog. He felt like he would sail right over the edge of the world.

Stupid rain! Why did it have to be this way? Why didn't it stop? Everything had been fine until the rain came along and changed things.

Dashiell missed his scooter. He missed Nintendo DS and Game Cube. He missed Tom and Jerry, Johnny Quest, Speed Racer and Tobor the Eighth Man. He missed riding in the car with his Mommy, singing along to the songs on the radio. He missed playing with his sisters, and their clubhouse and secret

157

street—a never-developed cul-desac on the edge of the woods next to their house. He missed tennis lessons at the clinic, playing football, and helping his Dad in the yard.

Every time his father went out of town, Dashiell used to get very sad. Every night, he would ask his Mom when Dad was coming home.

He buried his rain-streaked face against his stuffed dog and asked it now.

Dashiell wished he was at home, in bed with his parents, snuggled up between them, warm and dry and safe. His legs grew more numb. His teeth were still chattering but he no longer noticed. Dashiell stopped kicking, and only the life vest kept him afloat. Dashiell tried to sing, but the words died in his throat. His voice was hoarse and weak. Despite his fears, Dashiell finally succumbed to exhaustion and exposure to the elements, and closed his eyes.

Splashes sounded in the darkness around him. The snaky things crept closer, and Dashiell slept.

Kevin and Taya Locke, and their Yorkie dog, Harley, had been adrift in the ark for what seemed like forever. Kevin had lost track of the days. It was hard to mark the passage of time when the days blurred into a gray, misty haze. The sun and the moon were just pale, silver discs, both barely breaking the gloom.

Just as God (or whoever it was that had spoken to Kevin) had promised, the Earth was flooded again. Kevin had finished the backyard ark just in time. As Lafayette flooded, the vessel rose up off its moorings and floated. Kevin, Taya and Harley got onboard. They'd stocked the boat with plenty of food, water, and medical supplies. Kevin would have offered Rudy and Rosa a place onboard, but they'd disappeared. Taya feared the giant worms had eaten their neighbors, but Kevin assured her that they'd probably gotten away. They sat inside the ark, safe and warm and dry. When the water levels reached the rooftops, the ark floated out of their neighborhood—and out of Lafayette.

Kevin had to admit, he was grateful to God. He still didn't understand why the Supreme Being had appeared to him instead of Taya or Pastor Chad or a million other believers, but it didn't really matter. They were alive. Most of God's promise had come to pass. They'd sailed far and saved many. They found refugees clinging to rooftops and cell phone towers, and helped them onboard. The survivors told horrible stories—the worms (which they already knew about), and things that were half-shark and half-human, and flying piranha, and vampire mermaids, and a giant, squid-headed creature that destroyed entire buildings in its wake. Perhaps the most bizarre was a white fungus that slowly turned matter into liquid.

So the prophecy was fulfilled—at least partially. God's final promise, that if Kevin built the Ark, He would give them a child, had not come to pass. They'd continued trying, even in the face of the apocalypse, but their efforts were still unsuccessful. Kevin thought about all of this as he stood on the deck, staring out at the churning ocean.

"Maybe I was crazy," he muttered. "Schizophrenic. Maybe it wasn't God after all."

Lightning flashed, bathing the water with blue light. Kevin spotted something on the crest of a wave—a flash of orange. A life vest. Gripping the rail with one hand, he trained his spotlight on it and gasped.

"Man overboard," he shouted.

Footsteps pounded across the deck. Several survivors helped him extend a long hook on a pole. They managed to catch one of the straps on the life vest and, working together, they pulled the castaway into the ark. It was a little boy. The group clustered around him.

"Give him some room," Kevin urged, pushing them back. He knelt over the boy, and the child opened his eyes.

"Hi," Kevin said. "Are you okay?"

Frowning, the boy stared at the faces looming above him.

"My parents said I'm not supposed to talk to strangers."

"Well, my name is Kevin. What's your name?"

"Dashiell."

"Now we're not strangers."

The boy blinked rain from his eyes. "Is this Heaven? Are my Daddy and Mommy here?"

"No," Kevin said. "But you're safe. Let's get you out of this rain, Dashiell. And find you some dry clothes. Are you hungry?"

Dashiell nodded. Then he glanced out at the ocean. "There are things out there. Monsters."

"Yeah," Kevin agreed. "There are. But you don't have to worry about them anymore. Like I said, you're safe now. We all are."

Locke's Ark sailed into the night with its new passenger, and when they reached the end of the world, they sailed on through into a new day.

STORY
NOTES

If you're interested, here are some tidbits about each of the stories you just read and where they came from and where they were written.

As I said in the introduction, most of the stories in this book are based on real people. In some instances, they are based on the same people who appeared in a similar short story collection called *The Rising: Selected Scenes From the End of the World*. Those people paid for the privilege of having a story written about them. Long-time readers know that the overall mythos which connects all of my written works is based on the theory of alternate realities, and different versions of the same person inhabiting each of those realities. You can think of the folks in these stories as alternate reality versions of their alter-egos from the other book. I'm mentioning this now, because I'll refer to it in a few instances below.

Also keep in mind that before writing the stories, I interviewed each person and found out a little more about them. Each of the stories was then crafted with those details in mind.

Locke's Ark:

In *Earthworm Gods*, Teddy, mentions "some nut in Indiana who was building an ark." When I learned that Kevin lived in Indiana, I knew that I'd found my nut.

I've always been fascinated with the story of Noah. What if God really did show up and tell someone to build a big ship? How would they deal with it? Certainly, their reactions would run the gamut from sheer terror to bewildered amusement. I tried to capture some of that here.

I'm fond of this story. I like how it bookends the collection (Kevin and his ark show up again in the last tale—as well as in *Earthworm Gods II: Deluge*). This was written in my backyard on a sunny day. The weather was much like it is in the story.

Night Crawlers:

And then the worms make their first appearance. I got the idea for this while night-fishing alongside the Susquehanna River. I caught a really big catfish and when I got home, the sun was coming up. Rather than going to bed, I wrote the first draft of this tale.

Up A Pole, Without A Paddle:

Even though it appears early in the series, this was actually the last story I completed for the collection. I was almost out of story ideas and wondered just what the hell I'd write about. I exchanged a few emails with Phil and he told me what he did for a living. All of the sudden, I had this image of a man on top of a telephone pole, with the worms all around and the waters rising.

I wrote all three drafts in a single night. And yes, the characters of Tim and Simon are a nod to my dear friends and fellow authors Tim Lebbon and Simon Clark.

On The Beach:

Stuart told me a bit about his family and where he worked. Nuclear, on both counts. A nuclear power plant, a nuclear disaster, and the archetypal "nuclear family"—what writer could pass up a chance to play with that symbolism? It's not a joyous ending, but it's as close to a happy ending as characters in my work get.

This was written over two days, within the shadow of the Three Mile Island nuclear power plant, which was just up the river from where I lived at the time.

Last Drop of Sorrow In A Blue Bottle:

Bob Ford is a good friend of mine. He writes under the name Robert Ford. This story, and its title, feature elements from his first published chapbook (which you should read if you can find one for sale online). The chapbook contains the stories "Bluebottle Summer" and "Free Ride Angie." Obviously, you can see how they fit here. Bob also knows about the muse, and the altar on which writers often make sacrifices to it. We've had many late-night talks about that very thing, and I wanted to include some of that here.

I wrote this in my office after drinking some fine rum that Bob left behind on his last visit.

Swept Away:

Chris and Fran appeared in *The Rising: Selected Scenes From the End of the World* with their story, "Best Seat In The House". Their love really is the good and all-too-rare kind that most folks never get to experience in life. I did my best to capture that with their previous story, and had intended to do the same with this one. Then Chris told me to, "throw in some sex and make it hot as hell." So I did.

I don't write a lot of sex scenes. There's one in *Dark Hollow* and one in *Kill Whitey*. But when I write these sex scenes, I often get embarrassed. I'm not sure why. I love sex. I'm not a prude and I'm anything but vanilla. And writing descriptive passages of decapitations and disembowelments doesn't faze me. Despite this, writing about two people having sex always makes me squirm. But I like how this one turned out.

This story was written over two hot days in June, while I sat alongside my trout stream. I caught three fish. Chris died with a smile on his face. Everyone was happy.

Run To The Hills:

This story was originally published in two parts. Part one was from Paul's perspective and part two was from H's point-of-view. I merged the two tales together for this volume. Paul and H also appeared in *The Rising: Selected Scenes From the End of the World*. In those stories, Paul became a zombie and attacked H. The ensuing battle destroyed them both, along with H's legendary book collection. Both of them enjoyed the bizarre team-up, so when I got the chance to write about them again, I asked them if they'd like to join forces once more. This time, none of H's books were damaged.

I wrote these at home, in my office, and giggled the whole time.

Floating Home:

Not much to tell about this one. I wrote it in a hotel room in Minneapolis/Saint Paul, during a really bad thunderstorm. Good ambience. Terry appeared in *The Rising: Selected Scenes From the End of the World*. In that book, I killed his dog, Woody. I've always felt bad about that, so this time, Terry got to protect Woody, and they had a happy ending (something that rarely happens in my stories). I feel less guilty now.

The First Principle:

If *Earthworm Gods: Selected Scenes From the End of the World* has a core story, it is this one (along with its sister story, "The Final Principle"). Mark's broadcasts echo across many of the other tales in this volume. See if you can spot them all. They also have an impact on the events in *Earthworm Gods II: Deluge*.

The title and the ideas behind it stemmed from a late-night conversation I had with author and professor Drew Williams. We were sitting around a campfire, drinking good bourbon and discussing philosophy, and he told me about Thales' theory. And just like that, everything clicked. This is the result. And it makes perfect sense within the confines of this fictional setting.

I wrote this story at 3am, when the world was dark and quiet. The character of O'Neill is a nod to my friend and peer, science fiction and horror author Gene O'Neill.

In The Shadow of Taranaki:

Mean also appeared in *The Rising: Selected Scenes From the End of the World*. In the afterword to that collection, I relate a story Mean told me about New Zealand's opossums. He said: "We had an old single shot .22 rifle mainly for rabbits and opossums. Our opossums are not like your possums there in the States. Our opossums may make good zombie stoppers, as they don't actually attack people—but when they get frightened, they consider people are like trees and climb them and wrap themselves around your head. They have very long sharp claws, prehensile tails, are incredibly strong, and don't smell too good. Removal is a difficult process, to say the least."

Needless to say, I really, really wanted to use New Zealand's opossums in a future story. When I found out Mean would be in this book, I finally got my chance.

Riding The Storm Out:

The idea for this story also came from author and professor Drew Williams. (It occurs to me that perhaps Drew is my muse, and that makes me uncomfortable in ways that I can't even begin to describe). The legend of The Flying Dutchman is fascinating and one of my personal favorites. I'd love to write a novel about it one of these days.

This story was written in my backyard while I watched a thunderstorm roll in over the mountains.

Bad Fish:

This story introduces one of many new additions to the *Earthworm Gods* bestiary—flying, carnivorous fish. Poor Brian Lee got killed by zombie plants and insects in *The Rising: Selected Scenes From the End of the World*. He gets killed by man-eating fish this time. Dude's got no luck. If I ever do another of these books, I'll have to let him live.

Loads and Loads:

An astute critic once pointed out that parenthood—especially fatherhood—is an ongoing theme in much of my work. I'd say that's pretty accurate. When I wrote this story, I had a 16-year old son and another son on the way (now, as I write these story notes, the oldest is 21 and the one who was on the way just turned four not too long ago). My history with my own father is complex, as is his history with my grandfather. And yes, a lot of that finds its way into my fiction. I thought I was done talking about fathers and sons way back in *City of the Dead*, but the theme popped up again in *Ghoul, Dead Sea, Dark Hollow*, and *Clickers vs. Zombies*, and has popped up in other works, too, including this story.

Of all the stories in this book, I think this one is my favorite. I wrote it in one sitting—from midnight to six in the morning, all three drafts. When I was finished, I felt drained—but good. I've always hoped that Stephen enjoyed it as much as I did. As this book was being proofread in advance of its new paperback and digital release, pre-reader Mark 'Dezm' Sylva (he of the radio broadcasts in Boston from "The First

Principle") sent me this note: *I know for a fact that Stephen enjoyed it immensely. Me and him email each other weekly talk about our sons, etc. Every time when he knows I'm going to hang out with you at a convention or signing or something he always says, "Make sure you tell Brian I said hello and that Loads and Loads is still my favorite story by him!" He's actually got the manuscript framed and hanging in his living room. And he frequently quotes the last line of the story. He's more happy with that story than you could possibly imagine. Hell, I think it's my favorite story in the book, too!*

As a writer, that's about the best thing someone can ever tell you about something you wrote. That is what makes this job worth it.

Message In A Bottle:
In this story, Mike is listening to Mark Sylva's broadcast (from "The First Principle") at the beginning, but then a second narrative introduces itself when Mike finds the note. I've always like the story-within-a-story device, and I rarely get a chance to use it.

This story was written in my office during a Godzilla DVD marathon, which explains the giant monster. The beast also showed up in *Earthworm Gods II: Deluge*. As for the creature—what is it? I don't know. It's not Leviathan or Behemoth, nor is it one of the smaller worms. Maybe it existed in the depths of the ocean before the rains started…and maybe I'll write about it again, one day.

The Magi:
Originally, I'd started a different story for Leigh and Penny. But when I found out that Penny was pregnant, and that they'd like their stories to reflect that, I scrapped the original idea and went with this instead.

More links to my overall mythos pop up in this story. We've seen Black Lodge appear in *Clickers III, Clickers vs. Zombies*, and my short story "The Black Wave". They are referenced in *Dead Sea, Ghost Walk*, and *A Gathering of Crows*. They are a black-ops military group who specialize in the supernatural—sort of like Rambo meets The X-Files. They play a major role in several upcoming novels, and lurk between the pages in many of my others. Careful readers will pick up some more clues from these two stories—but their true origins and goals are still unknown, except to me.

And, of course, Simon in *Earthworm Gods II: Deluge,* is a Black Lodge agent. He even mentions Leigh and Penny in that novel, and hints at what his fellow agents are going to attempt.

Take Me To The River:

Not much to say about this one. As stated in the introduction, it originally appeared in the special Lettered Edition of *Earthworm Gods.* The refrain of "Soft" that the fungal zombies are so fond of using as a mantra is a nod to F. Paul Wilson, someone I've admired since I was a teen, and who has been both a mentor and a dear friend in my adult years. (Paul is not the only writer whose work has inspired this series. If you look closely you'll see nods to William Hope Hodgson and Joe Lansdale in *Earthworm Gods* and *Earthworm Gods II: Deluge,* as well).

The End of Solitude:

In real life, Jade ran a small press outfit called Solitude Publications, and published books by myself, Tim Lebbon, Geoff Cooper, John Urbancik, Brian Knight, Shane Ryan Staley, and Mark McLaughlin. She's also a woman who values solitude—especially if it's the end of the world. So I wanted this story to reflect that and explore just how far someone would go to retain it.

I wrote the first draft at my veterinarian's office while my dog and my cat were getting their teeth cleaned.

Best Laid Plans:

The title and idea for this story came from some emails I exchanged with Scott. The inherent danger with using the fungal zombies in a story of their own is that they are similar to other zombies—and Lord knows I've written enough about them. While working on this story, I made a conscious effort not to repeat myself. Hopefully, I achieved that.

The Sky Is Crying:

Like myself, Jason is a big fan of the blues, especially songs from the pre-war era. He had a story appear in *The Rising: Selected Scenes From the End of the World*, in addition to the story that appears here. Both tales got their titles from classic blues songs.

This story also features the return of the Black Wave, a possibly man-made organism—indeed, there are hints that the mysterious Black Lodge may have been behind its creation—which first appeared in my short story "The Black Wave." (How's that for an appropriate title?)

Dawn of the Dorsals:

This story features another creature to the Earthworm Gods bestiary—half-human sharks. They are mentioned briefly in *Earthworm Gods* and make a full appearance in *Earthworm Gods II: Deluge*.

This story was a lot of fun to write. I only wish I'd have been allowed more pages. There was a lot I wanted to do with these creatures. Perhaps you'll see them again, elsewhere.

Date Night:

Another of my personal favorites in this collection. Tony and Kim had a story in *The Rising: Selected Scenes From the End of the World*, and I put them through the ringer in it. Seriously. As an author, I did some terrible, despicable things to their characters, which was hard, since I like them both very much in real life. They got a much happier ending this time around.

This story was written in one draft, after exchanging a few emails with Kim. I'm very happy with it. Hopefully they are, too.

Death By Cookies:

Although, out of necessity, I'm secretive about where I actually live, I have a public post office box (also out of necessity). Every day, I make a trip to the post office to see what people have sent me, and there's always something. Most of it is fan mail (I think it's cool that people still take time to write letters in the age of instant email) or movies, music, and other author's books that people think I might enjoy. I've gotten weird shit, too. Death threats. Screwy business offers. One particularly odious individual once sent me a dead bird. I also get a lot of food, which sadly, I don't eat. I appreciate it, but after you've received a dead fucking bird with your latest death threat, you're inclined not to eat food sent to you by strangers. The one exception to this is when Mark's wife, Paula, sends me a batch of her home-made cookies.

Let me tell you something, folks. I have experience with home-made cookies. My second ex-wife, my mother, my great-grandmother, both of my grandmothers, and all of my aunts know how to bake. So I think I speak with some authority when I tell you that Paula Beauchamp makes the best fucking cookies in the world. (Just don't tell my second ex-wife or mother that I said this). Her cookies could bring about world peace if we distributed them at the United Nations.

Her candy apples kick ass, too.

Serenade:

When people read *Earthworm Gods* (and "The Garden Where My Rain Grows") they had one of two reactions to the mermaid—love or hate. There are no neutral reactions to her character. The siren in this story isn't the same one from the novel. I always figured there were more of them spread across the ocean—each a bride of Leviathan. And this was revealed in *Earthworm Gods II: Deluge.*

Don Koish ran Necessary Evil, a fine small press publishing outfit. While writing this story, I grinned at the image of him riding around on a Jet Ski. If you ever meet Don in person, you'll know why. Dude looks like a pro-wrestler, but he's got the heart and personality of a puppy.

The Final Principle:

As I said earlier, if *Earthworm Gods: Selected Scenes From the End of the World* has a core story, it is this one (along with its sister story, "The First Principle"). Originally, the two stories weren't supposed to link. But when Steven told me what he did for a living, and requested that his tale take place in Boston, everything clicked. I'm really grateful to him for giving my muse the opportunity.

Liquid Noose:
Paul's one of my long-time readers, meaning he's been there since before the first book, back when my work appeared in small fanzines and webzines. We first met when Paul was running a newsletter for fans of Brian Hodge (whom we both rank right above Jesus, Mohammad, and David Lee Roth). Over the years, I've had many opportunities to hang out with him and Shannon, and I'm very fond of them both. They're no longer fans. They're friends—and family.

Like his story in *The Rising: Selected Scenes From the End of the World*, the title for this tale comes from one of Paul's favorite heavy metal songs.

The Chase:
This story's title serves double duty—it's the name of the skyscraper the story takes place in, and it's also the thrust of the plot. Most of *Earthworm Gods* various creatures make an appearance here—the man-sharks, flying fish, white fuzz zombies, etc. Writing it was a fun little adrenalin rush.

One Last Breath:
I wrote earlier about how fatherhood and parenthood are recurring themes in much of my work. Here they are again—a dark counterpoint to "Loads and Loads." This story is obviously continued in "Exodus A.D. (Locke's Ark: Reprise)."

Roman's daughters were both featured in *The Rising: Selected Scenes From the End of the World*. It was his son's turn this time around. Of all the stories in this collection, this one was by far the hardest to write—especially as a father. I'd like to think that Roman's heroic final act is one I'd repeat if I were in a similar situation.

The Last Ghost of Mary:

The tricky part was making this story different from "Riding the Storm Out." After all, both stories deal with ghost ships and nautical lore. This story, along with the two that follow it, make up the end of the Earth—or perhaps a new beginning. The clues are all there (and in the finale of *Earthworm Gods II: Deluge*). I leave it to you to find them.

At the Mountains of Melting:

The title is a play on the title of one of my favorite H.P. Lovecraft stories, "At the Mountains of Madness." The story itself ties into what was revealed in "The First Principle" and "The Final Principle." The world is liquefying.

A friend of mine, who happened to be visiting while I was working on this, said it sounded like one big acid trip. I think that's pretty apt. It's certainly more surreal than my usual work.

Exodus A.D. (Locke's Ark: Reprise):

In which all of our plotlines are wrapped up once and for all, and Roman's heroic last act bears fruit, and the promise God made to Kevin at the beginning of the book comes to pass. And unlike Jamie LaChance, these castaways are not ghosts, but alive. What will become of Earth's last survivors as they sail off into the sunset?

Well, if you've read *Earthworm Gods II: Deluge*, you might think you know. But do you really? Are you sure? Here's a hint: go back to the first story and re-read God's promise to Kevin—all of it. Did they really die in *Earthworm Gods II: Deluge*? Well, I know. I'm just not ready to tell yet. Suffice it to say, there is one more story to be told, and I'll write it one of these days.

I'll let you see it when I'm done…

Brian Keene

June 2012

173

BRIAN KEENE is the author of over thirty books, including *Darkness on the Edge of Town, Take The Long Way Home, Urban Gothic, Castaways, Dark Hollow, Dead Sea,* and *The Rising*. He also writes comic books such as *The Last Zombie*. His work has been translated into German, Spanish, Polish, Italian, French and Taiwanese. Several of his novels and stories have been developed for film, including *Ghoul, The Ties That Bind,* and *Fast Zombies Suck*. In addition to writing, Keene also oversees Maelstrom, his own small press publishing imprint specializing in collectible limited editions, via Thunderstorm Books. Keene's work has been praised in such diverse places as *The New York Times,* The History Channel, The Howard Stern Show, CNN.com, *Publisher's Weekly,* Media Bistro, *Fangoria Magazine,* and *Rue Morgue Magazine*. Keene lives in Pennsylvania. You can communicate with him online at www.briankeene.com or on Twitter at @BrianKeene.

deadite press

"Urban Gothic" Brian Keene - When their car broke down in a dangerous inner-city neighborhood, Kerri and her friends thought they would find shelter inside an old, dark row home. They thought they would be safe there until help arrived. They were wrong. The residents who live down in the cellar and the tunnels beneath the city are far more dangerous than the streets outside, and they have a very special way of dealing with trespassers. Trapped in a world of darkness, populated by obscene abominations, they will have to fight back if they ever want to see the sun again.

"Ghoul" Brian Keene - There is something in the local cemetery that comes out at night. Something that is unearthing corpses and killing people. It's the summer of 1984 and Timmy and his friends are looking forward to no school, comic books, and adventure. But instead they will be fighting for their lives. The ghoul has smelled their blood and it is after them. But that's not the only monster they will face this summer . . . From award-winning horror master Brian Keene comes a novel of monsters, murder, and the loss of innocence.

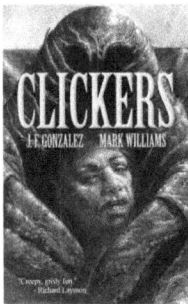

"Clickers" J. F. Gonzalez and Mark Williams- They are the Clickers, giant venomous blood-thirsty crabs from the depths of the sea. The only warning to their rampage of dismemberment and death is the terrible clicking of their claws. But these monsters aren't merely here to ravage and pillage. They are being driven onto land by fear. Something is hunting the Clickers. Something ancient and without mercy. *Clickers* is J. F. Gonzalez and Mark Williams' gore-soaked cult classic tribute to the giant monster B-movies of yesteryear.

"Clickers II" J. F. Gonzalez and Brian Keene- Thousands of Clickers swarm across the entire nation and march inland, slaughtering anyone and anything they come across. But this time the Clickers aren't blindly rushing onto land - they are being led by an intelligence older than civilization itself. A force that wants to take dry land away from the mammals. Those left alive soon realize that they must do everything and anything they can to protect humanity – no matter the cost. *This isn't war, this is extermination.*

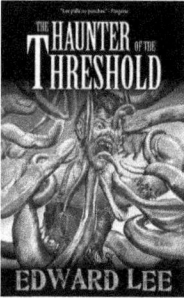

"The Haunter of the Threshold" Edward Lee - There is something very wrong with this backwater town. Suicide notes, magic gems, and haunted cabins await her. Plus the woods are filled with monsters, both human and otherworldly. And then there are the horrible tentacles . . . Soon Hazel is thrown into a battle for her life that will test her sanity and sex drive. The sequel to H.P. Lovecraft's The Haunter of the Dark is Edward Lee's most pornographic novel to date!

"The Innswich Horror" Edward Lee - In July, 1939, antiquarian and H.P. Lovecraft aficionado, Foster Morley, takes a scenic bus tour through northern Massachusetts and finds Innswich Point. There far too many similarities between this fishing village and the fictional town of Lovecraft's masterpiece, The Shadow Over Innsmouth. Join splatter king Edward Lee for a private tour of Innswich Point - a town founded on perversion, torture, and abominations from the sea.

"The Dark Ones" Bryan Smith - They are The Dark Ones. The name began as a self-deprecating joke, but it stuck and now it's a source of pride. They're the one who don't fit in. The misfits who drink and smoke too much and stay out all hours of the night. Everyone knows they're trouble. On the outskirts of Ransom, TN is an abandoned, boarded-up house. Something evil happened there long ago. The evil has been contained there ever since, locked down tight in the basement—until the night The Dark Ones set it free . . .

"Genital Grinder" Ryan Harding - *"Think you're hardcore? Think again. If you've handled everything Edward Lee, Wrath James White, and Bryan Smith have thrown at you, then put on your rubber parka, spread some plastic across the floor, and get ready for Ryan Harding, the unsung master of hardcore horror. Abandon all hope, ye who enter here. Harding's work is like an acid bath, and pain has never been so sweet."*
- Brian Keene

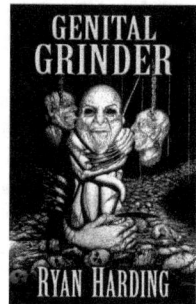

AVAILABLE FROM AMAZON.COM

deadite
press

"Brain Cheese Buffet" Edward Lee - collecting nine of Lee's most sought after tales of violence and body fluids. Featuring the Stoker nominated "Mr. Torso," the legendary gross-out piece "The Dritiphilist," the notorious "The McCrath Model SS40-C, Series S," and six more stories to test your gag reflex.
"Edward Lee's writing is fast and mean as a chain saw revved to full-tilt boogie."
- Jack Ketchum

"Bullet Through Your Face" Edward Lee - No writer is more extreme, perverted, or gross than Edward Lee. His world is one of psychopathic redneck rapists, sex addicted demons, and semen stealing aliens. Brace yourself, the king of splatterspunk is guaranteed to shock, offend, and make you laugh until you vomit.
"Lee pulls no punches."
- Fangoria

"Carnal Surgery" Edward Lee - Autopsy fetishes, crippled sex slaves, a serial killer who keeps the hands of his victims, government conspiracies, dead cops and doomed pornographers. From operating room morality plays to a town that serves up piss and cum mixed drinks, this is the strange and disturbing world of Edward Lee. From one of the most notorious, controversial, and extreme voices in horror fiction comes a new collection of depravity and terror. Carnal Surgery collects eleven of Lee's most sought after tales of sex and dismemberment.

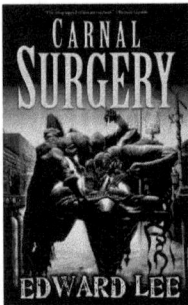

"Trolley No. 1852" Edward Lee - In 1934, horror writer H.P. Lovecraft is invited to write a story for a subversive underground magazine, all on the condition that a pseudonym will be used. The pay is lofty, and God knows, Lovecraft needs the money. There's just one catch. It has to be a pornographic story . . . The 1852 Club is a bordello unlike any other. Its women are the most beautiful and they will do anything. But there is something else going on at this sex club. In the back rooms monsters are performing vile acts on each other and doors to other dimensions are opening . . .

SACRIFICE
Wrath James White

All over town, little girls are going missing and turning up starved, dehydrated, and nearly catatonic. One man is eaten alive by his own dog along with half the pets in the neighborhood. An elementary school teacher is beaten to death by his own students while being stung by thousands of bees. It's up to Detective John Malloy and his partner Detective Mohammed Rafik to figure out how it's all connected to a mysterious voodoo priestess with the power to take away all of your hatred ... all of your fear ... all of your pain.

THE KILLINGS
J.F. Gonzalez & Wrath James White

In 1911, Atlanta's African American community was terrorized by a serial killer that preyed on young bi-racial women, cutting their throats and mutilating their corpses. In the 1980s, more than twenty African American boys were murdered throughout Atlanta. In 2011, another string of sadistic murders have begun, and this time it's more brutal than ever.

Down
Nate Southard

In 1992, The Frequency Brothers board a plane following a sold out concert in Austin, Texas. The plan is to fly to New York to shoot their next video. But then their plane goes down. Injured and stranded in a seemingly endless forest, The Frequency Brothers now find themselves fighting for survival. Everywhere they look, they see signs that they are not alone, that something waits in the darkness. They can hear it, and it sounds angry. There's something else out there, though. Something much worse. And it wants to drag them Down..

I'm Not Sam
Jack Ketchum & Lucky McKee

Now I'm way beyond confusion. Now I'm scared.
I've slid down the rabbit-hole and what's down there is dark and serious. This is not play-acting or some waking bad dream she's having. She's changed, somehow overnight. I don't know how I know this but I sense it as surely as I sense my own skin. This is not Sam, my Sam, wholly sane and firmly balanced. Capable of tying off an artery as neatly as you'd thread a belt through the loops of your jeans.
And now I'm shivering too.
In some fundamental way she's changed…

Lightning Source UK Ltd.
Milton Keynes UK
UKHW020901110920
369747UK00014B/1125